MW01128228

This book is a work of fiction. The names, characters, places, and incidents are products of the writer's imagination or have been used fictitiously and are not to be construed as real. Any resemblance to persons, living or dead, actual events, locale or organizations is entirely coincidental.

He knows how to sweep a girl off her feet, even ones who don't believe in romance.

With the Boot Knockers Ranch expanding to Montana, a whole new group of guys bust their butts on the ranch—and in the bedrooms. Foster has been many things in his life, but he's never been happier than as a Boot Knocker. Turns out all his sweet-talkin' and suave ways of his youth aren't wasted on the ladies who visit the ranch looking to experience the sexual thrill of a lifetime. He's charmed many a thong off a lady, though he's never faced a tough cowgirl like Chevy. She tries to ignore his charms, but they don't call him the Candlelight Cowboy for nothin', and there's no way he'll let her walk away less than satisfied. If she can walk at all.

Chevy is sick and tired of being romanced by fake men and then ditched when she gets attached. She's breaking the cycle—starting now. Finding the Boot Knocker who can help her seems like fate. He can work his magic all he wants, but she's in control. Knowing he's all talk means she holds the reins tightly. Or she's trying to. Foster's a master of wining, dining and 69ing. And don't even get her started on the moonlit horseback rides or bubble baths.

Foster makes every woman feel special, but with Chevy, everything is amplified. He needs to make her understand how amazing she is, or how can he go on? And Chevy thinks she must like punishment if she's falling for the same routine. But this is starting to feel so different…so true. Maybe like the least fake relationship she's ever had.

Cowboy by Candlelight

by

Em Petrova

Chapter One

"You know what they say — good on the ranch, better in bed." Foster threw his buddy and fellow Boot Knocker a grin.

Shayne gave a shake of his head. "How do you come up with this shit?"

"What? It's a saying." Foster paused in shoveling. Sweat poured off him in rivers. He could think of better ways to be spending his time than moving heavy earth at high noon. The sun beat down and it had to be at least ninety. Rare for these parts of Montana. The cattle on the Boot Knockers Ranch didn't like it any more than the cowboys did.

Shayne leaned on his shovel. "Who says it then?"

"Everyone in these parts. Ask Lil." Lil was the former owner of this ranch, but when she'd gotten in financial trouble and over her head with work, she'd accepted an offer from the Boot Knockers.

Since the Texans had a thriving operation and seemed to be raking it in, Foster thought she'd done well for herself. But she continued to work as hard as the rest of them.

"You just gonna stand there staring at the dirt? It ain't movin' itself," Foster ribbed his friend.

"Hot as Hades. The cattle can't even handle the heat. I swear I saw a bull go by carrying a fan earlier."

"Nah. It was one of those things that you wrap around your neck and it cools you down." Foster speared the earth with the point of his shovel.

Shayne chuckled and got to work too. Their hats at least offered some shade, but Foster could feel the sun tightening the skin on his shoulders.

"You boys are gonna get burned to a crisp." The familiar female voice brought them around to see Lil riding up. Seeing that horse and rider always gave Foster blue balls. Lil was sexy as hell, and the curvy blonde riding the black mustang was a sight not to be missed.

"I think we should start charging men to stop by the ranch and see Lil," he said.

"Very funny. Who would come to see me?"

Foster thought a lot of guys would shell out good money to watch a real ranchwoman like Lil. She was tough as nails and had beauty and the body to keep a man revving for days. But she was humble, and he liked that about her even more.

"Your backs are getting red. You should put your shirts on." She shielded her eyes from the glare of the sun and squinted at them.

"The ladies like the tans," Shayne said.

"No doubt. But how are you going to be on your backs all week when the new lot of ladies arrive?"

Foster's wicked grin came out to play again. He shot her a pointed look. "You think we're lying around letting the sweet women do all the work? Besides, plenty of positions you stand up for."

She rolled her eyes. "I don't know how you do it, but hats off to you." She picked up her hat and then set it back down on her shining blonde hair.

The ranch was more than cattle and hard work. Tomorrow they were expecting a new group of ladies who were coming to take advantage of the true function of the ranch — sex therapy.

If someone would have told Foster years ago that he'd put his sweet talk to good use, he would have guffawed in his face. It always surprised him to wake up next to a woman he'd just pleased to the point of a breakthrough. His last client had a hang-up about how she sounded when she had an orgasm. Foster taught her right quick that screaming was praise to her lover, and by the time she left, she was hoarse.

"Wipe that grin off your face and keep shoveling, cowboy," Lil interrupted his thoughts.

"You should give one of us Boot Knockers a try. Or several. Maybe one a day for two weeks. Think of that, Lil. You can sample the goods for free at any time."

"I didn't sell shares of my ranch so I could get free sex. Besides, shouldn't all sex be free?"

"The ladies aren't paying for sex. They're paying for help with their problems." Shayne backhanded sweat from his eyes.

"Yeah, I get it. I can't complain either. The Boot Knockers saved my ass, and I'm still standing here on my land with the herd my daddy started decades ago. Which is why I'm here to talk to you."

He and Shayne paused in their work to look at her. "Someone mentioned building more cabins along that ridge." She pointed, and they followed the direction of her finger.

"Yeah, heard that too," Foster said.

She shook her head. "No way. That's prime grazing land."

"Yeah, it's a goldmine. Build twenty more cabins and fill them with clients and Boot Knockers and who needs cattle?"

"I'm not amused, Foster."

"Dang, you're cute when you're riled." He saw his words achieved the opposite effect, and she glared at him. "Just kiddin'. Don't shoot me. Where do you propose the new cabins go?"

They were booked full and had a waiting list. They had sixteen resident Boot Knockers, but they cycled two off every week so they didn't burn out.

Or chafe.

"Now what are you grinning about, Foster? You have the attention span of a goat."

"Why you gotta go there, Lil? Haven't I been the nicest to you of all the guys? I do everything you ask me to around here."

"Well, now I'm asking you to tell the others not to build on that ridge. Hugh and

Riggs are coming up from Texas. Should be here any minute, and I don't want them giving the greenlight to the cabins."

Hugh and Riggs were the main bosses of The Boot Knockers Ranch in Texas. They'd worked alongside the guys for months until the operation started to run smoother. There were still kinks, but hell, they wanted lots of kink, didn't they? Doms, guys with fetishes, cowboys who only wanted anal. And a few that swung both ways, like Foster.

He wasn't picky about who he charmed the pants off, as long as he was having a good time.

"I didn't sell out to The Boot Knockers to run my ranch into the ground, and I need that land for grazing. Better finish up and get back to the lodge, guys. Hugh and Riggs will want to hold their usual meeting."

The Boot Knockers leased the land from Lil and paid her well, which meant they had a place to run their operation while she had the money and manpower to keep her beloved ranch afloat. Foster could see her point.

With that, she turned her horse and trotted away. Foster and Shayne watched her go, because it was too pretty a sight to ignore.

When her horse's hooves faded and she disappeared from view, they dug in and finished the job despite the heat.

By the time they got back to the ranch, Foster was ready for a shower, but things were already rowdy in the lodge. The whole group was there, and it seemed more like a rodeo than a meeting. Cowboys in worn jeans and dirty boots, many shirtless, but their hats all in place.

"See? We fit right in." Foster nudged Shayne and went straight for the fridge in the corner. The lodge had several large common rooms, and the dining area was equipped with plenty of drinks. He grabbed two bottled waters.

Shayne held up his hands as if to catch.

"Get your own. These're mine." Foster gave him a wink to soften his greed, and Shayne licked his lips in return. They shared a grin. Yeah, they'd slept together more than once. Shayne was a good lay, and Foster wouldn't mind a romp later today.

That was one thing about having constant sex—he wanted more and more. Several times a day too. In his off weeks, if he didn't find a couple to be their third, he turned to stroking himself.

Okay, so he was known for dropping his jeans and fisting his cock wherever he stood. Wasn't the point of the ranch about freedom to express their sexual tendencies? He liked giving a show, and there were many who liked his shows.

He leaned against one of the long tables in the space and drank off one bottle of water in a few gulps. He crushed it and moved to the second. Hugh and Riggs were a couple of cowboys like himself—they were in a committed ménage relationship with a sumptuous little blonde named Sybill. She'd come up to Montana a few times, but mostly she stayed home with their children.

Hugh spotted him and broke away from the group of guys he was bullshitting with. Foster offered his hand as he approached. Hugh was a big stud of a cowboy and definitely Foster's type. Riggs got a guy's blood pumping with those dark looks he gave out so sparingly. Too bad neither were into being with anybody but each other and Sybill.

Good thing the new ladies arrived tomorrow. Foster was so horny he'd jump anything at this point.

"How you doin'?" Hugh asked, shaking his hand.

"Lovin' life and can't complain."

Hugh nodded. "Good to hear we've got some dedicated guys up here in Montana. Look, I have something important to speak to Lil about in a while, and I'd like you there."

Foster rocked back a bit on his boots. "Sure. Why me?"

Hugh gave him a crooked smile. "You're known as the sweet talker of the group, right?"

"Yeah." They also called him the Candlelight Cowboy, because he loved to romance a woman right out of her bra and panty sets. He loved making ladies feel special with all the traditional ways they were taught to expect romance—candles, bubble baths, flowers, wine. He took it several steps further though by adding cunnilingus, skinnydippin', fuckfests and whipped cream.

"I might need you to lean on Lil a little bit for me," Hugh said, low.

"Now I'm intrigued."

Hugh gave a nod of farewell. "I'll call for you when the time comes."

Foster threw a look at Lil, who stood across the room, surrounded by Boot Knockers all vying for her affections. How she turned a blind eye to all that muscle, Foster didn't know. She must be a nun. Any other woman would be creaming her panties to be in the center of that group of studs.

Whatever Hugh had up his sleeve, one thing was sure. Lil wouldn't buy into it easily, and Foster had to get ready to persuade.

* * * * *

When Foster entered the office, Lil looked up from her seat across the table from Hugh and Riggs. Surprise showed on her face, and then she gave him a big ole smile.

He dropped into the chair beside her and stretched out his legs. She probably believed they were about to discuss the cabins and grazing land, and that he was on her side.

Which he was. Sorta. Both the ranch and The Boot Knockers were his life now—more than important to him. He didn't want to see the cattle pushed back so cowboys had more places to fuck.

"Thanks for coming, Foster, Lil." Riggs nodded to each. His confidence and good looks attracted everyone who spotted him.

Riggs relaxed against his chair back and eyed them. Lil fidgeted, but Foster waited to find out what his role was here.

"We had an upset when we arrived," Riggs said.

"Oh?" Lil raised a brow. "I hope it's not anything to do with my end of the ranch."

"No, you've made a lot of improvements, and we couldn't be happier with the way you're running things. We had to fire Miranda today."

She sucked in a gasp and Foster sat up straighter.

"Miranda the office manager?" Foster asked. She took care of everything to do with the clients who came here, from scheduling their visits to assigning them to the right Boot Knocker to arranging transportation for them to go home. Not to mention ordering supplies like condoms, lube, toys and a lot of rope that they seemed to go through like kids went through candy.

Hugh nodded.

"Why?" Lil asked.

"Sybill keeps a close eye on the books in this location, and she discovered something a week ago. Miranda was skimming off the profits."

Lil sucked in a gasp and Foster stiffened. He hated a cheat and thief more than anything. He was a plain, honest cowboy, and it grated on him when people weren't the same.

"Are you sure?" Lil set her fingertips on the edge of the table, and Foster saw they were white. She was pissed off too. Of anybody, Lil lost the most if Miranda'd been embezzling.

"Positive," Riggs said. "Seems Miranda had been skimming enough to open an account in Argentina."

Foster sat up. "A dummy account."

"That's right."

"Damn, just like the First National Bank of Chicago."

Everyone looked at him as if he'd grown a second head. He had more than enough heads to take care of without growing more.

"It's a famous case of embezzlement," he said. "Employees were making withdrawals from big accounts at the First National Bank of Chicago and transferring them to a dummy account in Australia. What's interesting about that case is the large amount they were able to steal before it was realized. How much we talkin'?"

Riggs named a number in the tens of thousands, and Lil launched out of her seat. She paced away, boots tapping to the beat of her anger.

"Don't worry, Lil. Sit and relax, please." Hugh waved to her vacant chair. "We've taken care of it, and every dime will be returned to our accounts within the week."

"How the hell did this happen, anyway? And how the hell do you know about the First National Bank of Chicago?" She turned her pale blue eyes on Foster.

Before he could speak, Riggs said, "I imagine he learned it when gaining his degree in finance."

Lil's jaw dropped. "What?"

"Didn't you know you have a master of finance shoveling your manure, Lil?" Hugh's amused tone echoed through the room. Foster sat back with a smile and enjoyed Lil's surprise.

"No," she said faintly.

"I believe Foster also holds a degree in history, particularly in the political side of things, am I right?" Hugh directed his question to Foster, who moved his hand in a wave of dismissal.

"And then there's the law school."

"What. The. Hell." Lil gaped at him as if she'd never seen him in her life. "Why the hell are you working here?"

He lifted a shoulder and let it fall. "I like the hard work and the peace."

Hugh and Riggs grinned as Lil continued to stare at him. He wasn't about to tell her he'd dabbled in technology too, and he could build a computer from a box of unused parts if he wanted.

She sank back to her seat and folded her hands in her lap. "So what do we do without an office manager?"

"We have a request of you, Lil." Hugh glanced to Foster.

Riggs plowed on before she could get a word in. "You know this place better than anyone, and we'd like you to take over until we can find a replacement for the position."

Lil didn't speak for a second, and Foster knew when she did that the sass would pour forth. He wasn't wrong.

"I know more about the land and cattle than anyone else, yes. But I don't know jack shit about The Boot Knockers' end of things. And do I look like I enjoy sitting behind a desk? Who's going to be running the ranch while I sit inside ordering dildoes?"

"See, you already know what we need," Foster jumped in, knowing why he was here. They needed him to convince Lil to take the job.

She started shaking her head, but he grabbed her hand and stroked her knuckles with his forefinger. She jerked free. "Don't think I don't realize what you're up to, siccing this sweet talker on me. Why don't you put *him* behind the desk?"

"We need you, Lil. It's only temporary."

"You're great at putting the guys in their place when we need it," Foster added. "Remember Blake?"

"Yes, I do. Damn pain in the ass. That's one incident, and I don't want to babysit a bunch of overgrown boys masquerading as cowboys."

"You're damn good at getting the best prices. I've never seen anyone negotiate a deal on feed the way you did," Foster went on.

"Oh, shut up," she snapped. She was relenting the more he complimented her prowess.

He gave her the eyes. He'd never had a woman escape that look yet, and Lil turned a bright shade of pink. He almost laughed. He could be a real dick if he wanted to, but this was in the name of business. And she'd get over it—she was good-natured. Probably kick his balls later, though.

He changed tactics and went for the kill. "We need a firm hand, Lil. I wonder if you can handle us." He let go of her fingers and kicked back with his boots propped on the table.

She smacked his thigh. "Get your feet down and be respectful, you ass. Fine! I'll take the job, but for no more than two weeks."

Riggs and Hugh grinned. "That should be time enough to find a replacement. Thank you."

They didn't direct the thanks to Foster, but he saw they were pleased with the outcome. He got up and caught Lil by the hand, drawing her to her feet. He kissed her fingers, letting his lips linger on her skin.

"I'll see you later, boss, when I come in to order my extra-extra-large condoms."

She yanked her hand free and swung at him, but he ducked. As he walked out of the office, he adjusted his cock to fit better in his Wranglers. Just having a woman's soft skin under his mouth had made him hard.

He couldn't wait to meet his next girl.

Chapter Two

Chevy ran her gloved fingers down the length of the foreleg. She concentrated on the bones and tendons within the horseflesh. Royal Ribbons had been favoring one leg lately, and she'd checked it several times.

"I must be missing something," she muttered to the horse. It didn't make a sound or move a muscle as she squeezed and manipulated the leg.

"Why don't you call that vet in?" Her sister stood a few feet away scattering fresh hay in the stall of their new momma and foal, who were out in the paddock enjoying the sunshine right now.

Chevy looked up at Sadie. "You can't be serious. That asshole?"

"What's wrong with him?" Her sister twisted to look at her. Her blank expression shifted, and she said, "Ohhh. You fucked him."

"Dated him." She didn't want to be reminded of the mistakes she'd made, and she'd made plenty.

"You were so into him at first. What happened?"

"Same thing that happens with every guy I date. They're players. After a few weeks I see their true colors, and I have to dump their stupid asses."

"After you've slept with them, fallen for them and dreamt of all the babies you can raise together."

"Shut up." She closed her eyes to concentrate on the lines of the tendon under her fingers, but mostly to get away from the conversation. If digging a hole and climbing in would help her forget all the douchebags she'd been with over the past two years, she'd grab a shovel right now.

Sadie didn't say more, but she didn't have to. Chevy was thinking about it enough on her own. Her sister wasn't wrong. Chevy had a tendency to fall for a line like a pig swallowed leftovers. She had a radar for men who acted like they'd treat her well—and then treated her like crap.

If she could only figure out how to unplug that radar and go for a normal guy. But the ones she met seemed dull. She hated to admit it to herself, but she loved being swept off her feet by the warm fuzzy emotions of a man being into her.

The vet Sadie had mentioned had served her champagne with her breakfast in bed, for God's sakes. Who did that? As she'd sipped her bubbly, she'd gotten drunk on the man. Turned out that after a few sleepovers, his attentive ways vanished and he'd stopped returning her calls.

Chevy rarely held anything back from her baby sister, but she'd been too embarrassed by the latest with the vet to tell her. Besides looking like twins with the same warm brown hair that shone red in the sun, matching sets of brown eyes and too many freckles inherited from their momma, she and Sadie were best friends.

Soon something big would separate them, though. In six weeks' time, Sadie would have a different last name. Her baby sister was walking down the aisle with a guy Chevy thought of as a little vanilla and dull, but her sister loved him and that was all that mattered.

Now, why couldn't Chevy convince herself that a guy like her sister's fiancé would be great for herself?

"How's the leg?" Sadie leaned against the stall door, pitchfork in hand.

Chevy sank back in her crouching position and sighed. "Don't know. Wish I did."

"Why don't I call the vet? You can hide in the house."

"Ugh. I never hide."

Her sister giggled. "Is that what happened when the rancher's son up the road delivered that water tank to us last week? You were conveniently absent, sis."

Chevy pushed out a long stream of air through her nostrils and dropped her head back to stare at the wood beams above. "Why am I so stupid about men, Sadie?"

"Ohh, poor sissy." She came forward and dropped to the floor beside her. When she put her arms around Chevy, she didn't resist and leaned against her. "You're one of the smartest women I know, but you are a little naïve when it comes to guys. I was thinking Mike and I will find you a date for my wedding."

She leaned away from her sister. "What? No freakin' way."

"Why not?"

She started naming all the men she'd been with over the past year.

Sadie giggled. "You do fall for a line of BS, sis."

"I know that. It's why I've been thinking of doing something about it."

"Like deafen and blind yourself so they can't schmooze you? Oh wait, they'd use their hands. No deadening a sense of touch, Chevy. I think you're screwed."

Chevy got up and grabbed the abandoned pitchfork.

"What are you gonna do? Find a corpse? Men throw everything at you to get you. I never had that luck, but I did find a good one in the end."

Chevy turned in time to catch her baby sister's dreamy smile. She was truly happy for Sadie that she was starting her life with a man who suited her needs. Her mind skipped to the website she'd spent all week drooling over. She hadn't made up her mind to book the trip there, but it was high time she did.

She faced Sadie—took a deep breath of the hay-and-horse-scented air.

Her sister went still, knowing her well enough to guess something big was coming.

"There's a ranch that specializes in sex therapy."

Her jaw dropped. "You need that?"

"Hell no, but I need what they have to offer. They help women work through their relationship and sex problems, and I'm majorly fucked up, aren't I? I jump from jerk to jerk."

"You're a hopeless romantic, Chevy. You—"

She threw out her hand. "Ugh, don't even use that word to me. The last thing I want to be is a romantic sap. I'm a hard-ass cowgirl who doesn't even need a man."

"Soo… what does the sex therapy place do for you?"

"There's a guy there." The picture of the man filled Chevy's mind. "Tall and dark-haired with a wicked glint in his eyes and a smile aimed to rip a woman's clothes off. Exactly my type—and the reason I need his help."

Her sister shook her head, not understanding.

"He's known as the Candlelight Cowboy, and that's who I'd stay with."

Sadie's eyes rounded. "To do what?"

"He wines and dines me and I practice saying no to him. I'll know he's BSing me, that what he's saying can't be real because we're strangers."

23

"And you think this will break the cycle?"

"Yep." It seemed the only course for her now. She had to grow the girl-nads to stand up to men who wanted to woo her. If they came at her with honeyed words, she'd throw up a shield. She'd resist flowers and jewelry they offered like a queen sending a subject to his execution.

And the Candlelight Cowboy would give her practice.

She nodded, deep in thought. As soon as she went inside, she had a date with her laptop and would book a spot on The Boot Knockers Ranch.

The Candlelight Cowboy didn't know what he had coming to him. The image of his rugged good looks hung before her mind's eye.

He sure was pretty to look at. At least she'd find some satisfaction in the deal.

* * * * *

When Foster walked into the office, he found Lil slumped over a desk strewn with papers and her lower lip caught in her teeth in concentration.

"You sure look cute as office manager."

24

She didn't look up. "Shut it, Foster. You're the reason I'm in order form hell." She collapsed face-down on the desk with her arms flung out to the sides.

He chuckled and approached the desk with caution. Lil was stressed, and much like cattle, a stressed woman could turn and charge at you without warning. He wasn't about to tell her he was comparing her to livestock in his mind, though.

He hitched his ass cheek onto the corner of the desk and stared down at her. "Whatcha orderin'?"

"Anything and everything." She sat up and leaned back in the leather chair with exasperation etched on her face. She waved a hand over the desk. "Produce, more bedsheets because somehow they're getting holes in them."

His lips twitched up, but he didn't say a word.

She glared at him before going on. "Guest shampoo and lotions. I've been doing this job for three weeks and I still haven't figured out what the fuck warming oil is and why we need it."

"Want me to show ya sometime?"

"Hell no. Flowers, candles, bubble bath." She picked a paper and read off it, "A twelve-inch super vibe with tickler attachment."

"Oh, that's for Wyoming." Their fellow Boot Knocker hailed from the state and had charmed his way onto the ranch by saying he knew everything about geysers and could make a woman gush like nothing they'd ever seen.

"Perverts—all of ya." Lil flashed her first smile. "This is overwhelming. Plus, I have the transportation group we use to collect the new group of women from the airport calling every five minutes to ask another question. This is all on top of me having a guy coming by later to speak to me about buying fifty head of beef to supply his restaurant in Seattle. How did the last office woman manage all this?"

He leaned over the desk and plucked a paper free. "Can you order me some erotic soybean candles?"

"What the hell are those?" She ripped the paper free of his grasp and smashed it onto the surface with one palm. She grabbed a pen and looked ready to stab the paper to death.

He got off the desk and circled behind her. As soon as he laid hands on her shoulders, she groaned. He kneaded the knots along her shoulders and up her neck. "This is what the candles are for. You light them and the jojoba oils can be used for massage." He lowered his lips to her ear. "Erotic massage."

She slapped at him. "Cut that out. I'm not your next conquest."

Laughing, he went back to his corner. "I also need some wildflowers from the florist."

"Not red roses?"

"Nothing so sappy, no. The woman I have coming this week is a country girl if I've ever seen one. She's got wildflowers written all over her."

"You're good at your job, Foster."

He laughed and reached out to direct a stray tendril of hair away from her cheek. "You don't know the half of it, darlin'."

When she slapped him this time, she made contact. His hand stung, and he yanked it back.

"Why are you here anyway?" Lil pressed. "You're smart, have all those degrees. Why would you want to break your back with hard work and play with all these women who won't ever mean anything to you?"

He sobered. "Just because I won't end up in relationships with them doesn't mean they

27

don't mean anything to me. I remember every single one. I like helping them, seeing them change and grow in just a week under my... tutelage."

At that, she laughed. "Okay, I get it. But why don't you want to go use the degrees you worked so hard for?"

"Tried on all those jobs. Didn't love any of them. Then I took a summer off and worked as cowpoke. I'd never been happier, and I've never looked back."

"You can't do this forever, though. Don't you ever wanna get hitched?" She stared up at him.

"Nope. You?"

"Nope." She smacked the desk lightly for emphasis.

"Got plenty of thongs off in my day, though. You wouldn't be wearin' one right now, would you?"

Her look was aimed to kill. Laughing, he circled the desk and moved to the door. "Order the stuff for me? Thanks, doll."

"Shut the door on your way out! I don't need more of your kind bugging me while I'm trying to work," she called after him.

He was still chuckling when he went outside.

"Tell me you didn't get in to see Lil." The familiar drawl made Foster turn. Wyoming was coming at him with a sideways grin.

"Yeah, just came from there." Foster appraised his buddy's state of wear. His shirt hung open and his hat was askew. He'd definitely just come from the barn, judging by the state of his boots. But Foster's guess was Wyoming wasn't working out there.

"Every time I poke my head in the office, Lil throws shit at me."

Foster's grin widened. "She's stressin' pretty hard right now."

"I'll give her something hard."

Foster reached out and cupped the bulge in Wyoming's jeans. "Feels ready."

"Haven't gone down yet. Just found Shayne and his woman in the barn. Passed her between us then shared her. This your free week?"

Foster nodded. "Feelin' the effects too."

"You shoulda hit me up." Wyoming pinched Foster's nipple, and electricity and arousal zipped through his body. "You know I have a soft spot for you, Fos."

He edged closer till his body was plastered against Wyoming's, muscle to muscle. Damn, he loved a good romp with this Boot Knocker. And he was the best third on the ranch, for sure.

"I'll see if my new lady's into some extracurricular activity." He felt along the line of Wyoming's cock, many inches that flared into a swollen head somewhere along his belt.

Wyoming leaned in and stamped a kiss on Foster's lips. "You know where to find me. I gotta talk to Lil, no matter what she hurls at my head."

Foster let his eyelids droop. "See ya 'round." He let go of his friend's crotch and they headed in opposite directions. A few steps away, Foster glanced back, only to find Wyoming doing the same. He tipped his hat to Wyoming and they shared a grin.

Now Foster was so fucking hard he couldn't wait to find someone to toy with. A week off was always a hardship for most Boot Knockers, and he was beginning to feel downright deprived. He'd sat in on the BDSM munch and played a bit. He liked the group sex as much as anybody else, but he missed the one-on-one with a partner.

Call him old-fashioned, but he got something from the intimacy of having a woman in his bed. Talking to her, stroking her hair, listening to her talk about her hopes and dreams.

Then climbing on top of her, pinning her arms overhead and sliding his cock balls-deep.

Oh yeah, that was what he needed right now. Too bad Lil was so damn grumpy or he might turn around and put on his best smile. Hell, he'd pull out the smoldering look that won every woman into his arms.

Four days until his client arrived—a Miss Chevy Daniels from a few counties over. Usually the Boot Knockers didn't get their client files until a day before they arrived, but Foster had gotten bored waiting around this week and snooped in Lil's office. He had to admit when he'd opened the file and spotted the beauty's photo in the upper corner, his jaw had dropped.

It wasn't that they didn't get beautiful women on The Boot Knockers Ranch, but Chevy was exceptional. All big brown eyes and freckles to win a man's heart. He'd looked away from her cowgirl hat perched on brown hair long enough to read her reason for coming to the ranch.

Ready for some wooing.

She'd picked the right guy. Right away, he'd thought of five ways to make her heart skip, to give her that special glow before he laid a hand on her.

Too bad she wasn't here right now. He'd like to see how he could affect her... whether those freckles stood out more when she blushed.

His cock was hard thinking about a flush on her peachy-soft skin. He nudged it into a better position. Damn, he needed to find some relief, even if it was sitting in a corner watching.

That sparked an idea. He headed toward cabin 9. Shayne liked having an audience, and his woman of the week was a wild one. With luck, she'd enjoy putting on a little show.

Chapter Three

Chevy's nerves were too jittery, and she'd bitten off all her nails on the way to the ranch. It had taken a supreme act of will to keep from primping for this week. Knowing she'd be with a sexy hot stud of a cowboy brought out her urges to doll herself up. But her reason for coming here was at complete odds with this female stupidity, so she'd pushed it away.

Although, she *had* waxed everything she could possibly wax. She might be looking to put an end to a bad cycle in her life, but she wasn't about to do it looking like a Yeti.

Riding in the back seat of the car bringing her to The Boot Knockers Ranch made her feel uncomfortable. She wasn't used to being driven like this, and she would have liked to sit up front and get a good look at everything.

The sprawling land stirred her. The ranch where she lived and had grown up was more mountainous while this one had beautiful hills, mountains and green fields that made her eyes sting at the brightness.

They passed through a set of huge gates constructed of log and steel. In the center of both was a brand she didn't recognize.

"Is that the Boot Knockers' brand?" she asked the driver.

The ordinary man dressed in plaid shirt, jeans, boots and hat smiled at her in the rearview mirror. "Nope, that's Miss Lil's family brand."

"Miss Lil?"

"She inherited this ranch from her family but struggled to keep it afloat. She took on the Boot Knockers."

Interesting that he didn't say the Boot Knockers took her on. This Miss Lil must hold the reins and control around here. Chevy found herself liking her sight unseen — she always rooted for a strong woman.

That's what I'm here to become. I can't let men rule me anymore.

The road leading to the ranch curved, and she sat up straighter as a huge ranch house came into view.

"That's the main lodge, where you'll come to eat. Also, there's activities." His tone held a note of amusement.

"I imagine some extraordinary activities."

He tossed his head back with a laugh. "You got it, Ms. Daniels. Here's your welcome committee now." He pulled to a stop, and

34

before she could look around, the back door opened and she was staring at a muscled midsection. The cowboy who ducked to look in at her shocked the life out of her.

She stared. Surely this man wasn't Foster, the guy she was spending the week with. He was too big, too hunky. Larger than life.

Suddenly shy, she could only stare at him and thanked God that she wore sunglasses and he couldn't see her eyes.

He threw her a crooked grin that sent a spark of awareness through her. When he reached a hand through the door, she snapped herself out of it.

She contemplated his hand — tanned, big-knuckled, callused from hard work. The old her would have taken that hand and melted at how it felt wrapped around hers, imagining it on her bare skin.

But the new Chevy didn't take his hand at all.

Ignoring it, she swung a boot out of the car and settled it on the ground. He stepped back to let her out. A whistle sounded from the porch area, followed by a holler. "Damn, we need to start fightin' for these girls the way they do down in Texas. I'd push my button over that one."

Foster didn't respond, but she saw his jaw tighten.

Did that mean he was into her? That he'd battle it out to keep her?

A seed of warmth bloomed in her stomach.

"I'm Foster, and in case you're wondering what that jar-head up there's jawin' about, The Boot Knockers Ranch in Texas has an auditorium where they fight over the girls they get for the week."

"I know."

"You do?" Even the cock of his dark brow set her stomach aflutter. Damn, damn, damn! She had to throw up a brick wall around herself, a no-bullshit fortress that would keep her from falling for how good those low-slung jeans looked on Foster right down to the way his deep voice hooked her.

"I read up on both ranches before making my choice."

His grin was a gorgeous thing. Wide, full lips and crinkles at his eyes.

Easy, Chevy. Down, girl.

He fingered the brim of his black hat and lowered his head—and his voice. "Must mean I beat all The Boot Knockers for the best girl, then."

She opened her mouth to say something that was far too much like the old Chevy. She checked herself. "I have some luggage."

He straightened, staring. She walked to the trunk, which the driver had popped. She started to reach for her bag, but Foster moved around her and grabbed the handle.

"I can get my own bag," she said, shoving her sunglasses back on her head.

Their gazes locked like a missile on a target. Only she didn't know which she was. Foster was definitely heat-seeking, and if she didn't drop off the radar quickly, her plan would end up blown to smithereens.

"It's our jobs to make sure you're taken care of while you're here, Chevy."

Fuck, did he have to say her name like that, so sweet? And he could definitely lose that grittiness in his voice. And why did she even notice things like that? She had a sickness.

She didn't release the bag, and neither did he. They stared at each other.

"Let me take the bag." His lips were twisted, but in annoyance or amusement? She didn't want him to think of her as a stubborn little—

Wait. Why do I care what he thinks? I'm paying him to help me see through his crap.

She wrenched the bag away from him and slung the long handle over her shoulder.

"All right then. A woman who knows her mind is mighty sexy." He was at her ear, his voice seeping into her brain.

He smelled good too, like cologne and fresh air. She'd have no trouble getting naked with this man. Steam was starting to come off her at his nearness.

"This way," he whispered, raising the small hairs on her neck with his breath.

He led her away from the lodge and around back. The path was paved with smooth stone, and it must have cost a fortune just to lay it. She looked ahead and saw the path meandered to a group of small log cabins, miniature versions of the lodge with red front doors.

"We're in the third one." Foster pointed. "Did you have a good trip?"

"Not bad. The ranch is beautiful."

He gave a single nod so manly that her sex clenched in reaction. *So that's the way of it. Lust I can deal with.* Rather than fight her instincts, she'd roll with them.

"One of the most beautiful spots of land I've ever seen, let alone lived on," he said, walking ahead of her to the door. He pushed it open and cool air scented with wildflowers wafted out. Her favorites. How did he know? Or were all the cabins dressed with wildflowers?

Either way, it was a nice touch, one the old Chevy appreciated very much.

He turned to her with a smile meant to scorch her panties off.

It almost worked.

Okay, so they were only singed.

"How's your ranch compare?" he asked.

She stepped inside, and he closed the door behind them. She glanced at anything but the striking man she was meant to stay with in this cabin. And sleep with. So far he wasn't pitching anything she couldn't bat away, but he surely had the nickname of the Candlelight Cowboy for good reason.

"My ranch is beautiful too, but the fields here are much bigger."

He nodded. "Been up your way a few times. Worked in Missoula a while before coming here."

"We're south of Missoula."

"South you say?" He pitched his voice low and stepped toward her. Her nipples bunched at the heat he threw off, and she set her bag down to distract herself from the strength in Foster's body and the lights dancing in his eyes.

"Are you too tired to take a walk? See the ranch?"

She reached for the buttons on her denim shirt with the embroidered pockets. "Nope. Let's just get down to business."

* * * * *

The second Chevy had pushed her sunglasses back and he'd seen those big brown eyes, he'd felt a fist in the gut. It remained tightly clenched all the way up to the cabin. But seeing her elegant fingers working her own pearl shirt buttons had his balls drawn up so tight they might never drop down.

"Wait. You want to hop in bed right now?" He was confused as hell by this woman. He saw that he affected her when he got close. But

40

then she'd stiffen and her words would come out clipped.

"Uh-huh." She unbuttoned the final button, revealing a simple black bra hugging a set of full, round breasts. She bent to pull off one boot. Then the other.

"We haven't even made it to the bedroom yet. This bodes well for our week, sweetheart."

Her eyes flashed with something he couldn't understand. Was it anger?

"I'm ready. Is the bedroom this way?" She turned and sashayed through the cabin, dropping her top as she went.

He gazed at her slinky spine and her long hair swaying over creamy, freckled shoulders. As much as he wanted to jump her, he needed to slow it down. This wasn't his way. He wooed. He kissed and romanced a woman into his bedroom. But Chevy was barreling in like she wouldn't get a chance if she hesitated to take a breath.

"Wait." He caught her at the door by wrapping his fingers around her bare upper arm. Her warmth… oh shit, he was fucking rock-hard now. He caught the trace of her body wash and just knew those vanilla-coconut scents would gather on her pulse

41

points. He wanted to bury his nose in her neck to find out.

She swung around to look at him, her lips far too enticing for him to resist. He bent to them. Brushed hers lightly.

She made a noise of surrender. Fuck, this was going too fast, but that sound undid him. He grabbed her around the middle and walked her backward to the bed while probing her lips with his tongue.

When he delved deep and tasted her for the first time, his cock jerked in his jeans. Lust was a hormonal reaction, and who was he to question science? He tugged her against his body, feeling her soft curves give in all the right places. As he raised his hands to cup her face, she grabbed his wrists and yanked them down to her breasts.

So ripe and firm. He swished his thumbs over the hard peaks, and they grew harder. Straining toward him as he swirled his tongue around and around her mouth. He strummed her nipples, and she moaned softly.

Five heartbeats hammered by before he drew back, dizzy with surprise that he'd let things get this out of hand. He was the professional, in charge. He was also the

Candlelight Cowboy, dammit, and she hadn't let him show off his abilities at all.

He drew a deep breath and put on the brakes.

She stared up at him with those big brown eyes hazy with need. She worried her lower lip between her teeth, and her breasts heaved into his palms with every breath she took.

"You're gorgeous and I want you straddling me and these in my mouth." He picked her up. She squeaked in surprise, and then he lay her on her back. All that brown hair tumbled across the covers. This just might be a record for getting a woman in bed. They hadn't been in the house two full minutes.

She swiped the hat off his head and tossed it aside. He grinned down at her and kissed her again while reaching beneath her for her bra clasp. He was a master with the things, and in seconds, the garment dangled from his fingertip.

"You're quick at that. Must have lots of practice."

One thing he hated was being ripped from the moment and reminded that this was his job. He especially disliked her thinking about it. The reason for her coming here, requesting him, was to be wooed to this state of high need.

Damn, she felt so fine beneath him, though. He broke the kiss to tear off his shirt. Then he made a dive for her again, trailing his lips around her delicate jaw to her ear. He worked over the shell with the point of his tongue for long minutes until she trembled.

When he hit a particular spot, she shuddered and moaned. So he languished over it even longer. Then he kissed a path down her throat to her breasts. The crests were so taut, so needy. He couldn't waste another second. He opened his mouth over one and sucked the point into his mouth.

As he pinched and rolled one nipple, he worshipped the other with his tongue. Soft mewling noises were escaping her, and he spread his palm over the flat of her belly, his pinky toying with her waistband.

How far did she want him to take it? How far before he stopped himself?

He was contemplating unbuttoning her jeans when she did it for him. She shimmied the denim down while rocking her hips upward.

The instant the small patch of brown curls was visible, Foster sucked in sharply. His cock fucking throbbed. He had to bury himself between Chevy's thighs and give them both satisfaction.

He sucked her other nipple and walked his fingers between her thighs to find her soaking wet center.

"Jesus," he grated out. "You're slippery as hell." He went for it—sinking a finger into her pussy and circling her taut nub with his thumb. Juicy noises filled the cabin, and his pulse drummed in his ears. As he clamped his lips around her nipple, he tormented her with his fingers.

When he added a second to her tight channel, he felt a tightening. A telltale sign that she wasn't going to last long riding his fingers. She bucked her hips.

"So fucking beautiful. Fuck my fingers, sweetheart. You're so slick around me."

"Ohhhh." Her drawn-out moan spiked his blood pressure. He had to get inside her or lose it like a virgin schoolboy.

He wanted to look everywhere at once. Her eyelashes fluttering on her high cheekbones, her lips parted in an O, her breasts rising with each panting breath she sucked in. And his fingers buried in her satiny heat.

She gripped at him with her inner walls, her thighs shaking.

"You're beautiful, open for me. I love seeing my fingers knuckle-deep in your pussy."

His words drew a groan from her, and she came for him with a sharp, feminine cry.

* * * * *

So fucking much for taking the upper hand. He'd ended up controlling her body with no problem and now he was running his finger under his nose, scenting her on him.

God, she was losing it already. Off balance. She needed time to think, and how could she do that with a gorgeous cowboy who'd just finger-fucked an orgasm out of her so big and forceful that she was still humming with sensation?

He leaned on one elbow, staring down at her, a gleam in his eyes and his lips quirked in a smile aimed to kill. She lost herself in his gaze for a minute before she jolted back to herself.

Damn, she was an idiot. One scorching look and a crooked grin could derail her, and here lay the problem.

He didn't want her, even if he knew how to command her body. Sure, he wanted to fuck her — she felt the evidence of that pressed against her hip.

He leaned in and claimed her mouth. The pressure startled her, and she made a hungry noise. Fuck, fuck, fucking fuck! She had no self-control, did she? No wonder she let the vet and ten other jerks walk all over her. Even if Foster wasn't a stranger and she were dating him, he'd do the same thing as those other guys — schmooze her panties off and then walk away.

What had her sister said? Guys threw everything at her in order to win her.

It was partly her reason for initiating sex right off the bat. If they got the fucking part out of the way, what was left? She'd easily dodge the honeyed words and shoot down whatever he planned to do with his stupid candlelight.

But as he thrust his tongue into her mouth, she felt herself sinking into the familiar dark waters of wanting.

She gripped his bulging biceps and parted her lips for more of his kisses. He threaded his fingers into her hair and tipped her head to receive him. Every pass of his tongue sent her into a higher state of arousal.

Hell, who was she kidding? It was frenzy. She scraped at his shoulders, but he seemed in no hurry to get between her legs. In fact, he lay completely still next to her, fully clothed except for his shirt hanging open.

He kissed her with a purpose that made her question everything she'd ever done with those other men. Because Foster knew how to *kiss*. This alone was worth the pricey week on the ranch. She could leave now, content with the price she'd paid for the experience.

No. What the hell am I thinking?

She was falling for it all over again.

She twisted from the kiss and pushed into a sitting position. He eyed her, a bemused smile on his rugged face.

"Sweetheart," he started.

She cut him off. "Maybe it's time for that walk." Except her pussy would throb with every step she took across the ranch. She *was* slipperier than hell. She'd come on his fingers, for God's sake.

48

She bounced to her feet, leaving him staring up at her. Sprawled on the bed, all six-foot-two inches of him, according to The Boot Knockers' website. His dark hair was too long at the nape and starting to curl, and his eyes scorched. He was sprouting a five o'clock shadow that made her clench her thighs together.

Suddenly, she realized she was nude in front of a stranger. Once again, all her clothes had fallen off for a man who obviously wasn't that into her.

When he sat up, he had ab muscles popping that shouldn't be there. She tried not to stare, but it was damn hard and she wasn't sure she succeeded. He was looking mighty smug.

She collected her clothing with as much decorum as she could muster after making a fool of herself. Then she went through a door into what she supposed was the bathroom.

"Uh, Chevy honey?"

"Yes?" She fumbled with her bra.

"That's the closet."

"I discovered that." Embarrassment rang in her voice, but there was nothing to do but continue to dress and suck it up. She could act like a ninny and leave the ranch after less than an hour or take the high road.

When she emerged from the closet, Foster was standing there holding his hat in his hands. She didn't know him well, but the creases between his brows told her things weren't going the way he'd hoped. How many other women did he see in a year? Probably none as bat-shit crazy as she was. Who came to a sex ranch with the sole purpose of saying no?

Their gazes met, and again that strange electricity zapped between them. Must be attraction, because she had no other word for it. She didn't know Foster from a hole in the ground.

"Still set on seeing the ranch?" he asked, turning the hat around in his hands.

"Yes." Somehow she managed to keep her tone clear and calm. "I'm looking forward to seeing everything."

"Okay, then. Your boots are here." He pointed to where he'd neatly placed them side by side next to the bed.

She had to pass him to reach them, and shyness and apprehension threatened to cripple her. But she pushed through the feeling and got her boots. He watched her put them on while he fastened his shirt buttons. The way his hands moved made her body ache to feel them on her again. In minutes, he'd robbed her of all sense and given her more satisfaction than she'd had in ages.

Maybe ever.

The way he kissed…

She straightened to her full height, which wasn't that much shorter than Foster now that she noticed. When he'd pulled her against him, she'd only been thinking about how well they fit together and how good his lips felt.

And before now, she hadn't bothered to glance at her surroundings. Turned out the room held more than a muscled body, a rough, angular jaw and dark eyes that burned deep into her.

"This place is nice."

"My favorite cabin. I like the…" He waved toward the pale blue-gray curtains. "What do you call them?"

"I don't know much about interior design, unless it involves horse stalls and places to store tack, but I think those are called curtains."

The corner of his lips twitched up, and the action seemed to be directly attached to her nipples. They hardened once again.

His gaze dropped to them, and he slipped a little closer. His fresh scent flooded her, dazed her. If she stood here long enough, she'd be under his spell again.

She clapped her hands and made a beeline for the door. "Wasting the day."

"I wouldn't call it wasted," he drawled from behind her.

She glanced back. "Are you looking at my ass?"

"Yeah, sugar. Nothing as fine as a woman's behind, especially when she keeps it fit in the saddle. What's your operation like?"

They went outside, and in the open air, she felt able to breathe again. In the close confines of the cabin, faced with Foster's glorious, chiseled chest, she battled for control. She hadn't gotten to touch him the ways she wanted, but what she'd felt was fine, fine, fine.

Maybe later she'd let things heat up a bit.

He caught up to her in two long strides and walked so close that their shoulders brushed occasionally. She saw through his act, though. He was trying to seduce her with his closeness.

Not happening.

When and if it did, it would be on her terms.

"My family has a spread of just under a thousand acres."

"Good size. Not too big to manage but large enough to keep a fair amount of cattle."

She nodded. This was territory she felt more comfortable navigating with Foster. "Keeps us all hard at work, and soon my sister's getting married. Her husband will be around to help, which is good since my daddy's slowing down a bit."

"So what color's the bridesmaid dress?" Foster's teasing voice worked at the edge of Chevy's mind, plucking at things she wasn't willing to give up. No sir, not this time around.

She shot him a smile at his question, though. "Maid of honor. And it's English tea."

"What the hell's that?"

She glanced around for something to compare it to, but the brilliant greens and rich browns were nothing like the color of her dress. Finally, she latched onto something to compare it to. "Like weak sweet tea."

"Ah." They walked a few more yards before he said, "Who wants weak tea?"

"Apparently my sister. It's not actually as bad as you'd think. Looks good with my boots too."

"Those boots?"

She looked down. "These are my I-can-work-and-still-look-good boots."

"And those are your my-sis-is-gettin'-hitched boots."

"Exactly." She gave a soft laugh despite how much she wanted to harden herself to Foster. He was cute and amusing.

"So how'd you get your name?"

She groaned. "I knew that was coming."

"Why?"

"Because everyone asks. It's not bad enough my parents saddled me with this name, but now I have to explain it to everyone I meet."

"Yup," he said, apparently not apologizing for his curiosity either.

She threw him a long look. He wore his hat slightly cocked and she wondered if he knew it. He seemed to have a habit of tugging on one side of the brim. "I'm sure you can guess."

"I have some ideas, but I want to hear it from your sweet lips."

Did he think her lips were sweet? She ran her tongue over them, and sure enough, he traced her movement.

Wait — what am I doing? Sweet-talker, remember?

She pushed out a sigh. "I was conceived in an old Chevy truck, okay?"

His smile did things to her insides—and outsides too. She liked those crinkles around his eyes too much, and the way his lips begged her to do bad things to him.

They're not begging. He's playing me.

"Wanna recreate the moment? We got an old Chevy pickup around here."

Thoughts of Foster tumbling her into the truck bed, their lips and tongues wild as they stripped off their clothes under the afternoon sun made her itchy to go find that truck. This was going to be one of many tests she faced this week. Time to give the correct answer.

"No thanks."

The groove was back between his dark brows, and if she didn't look away soon she'd want to smooth it with her thumb and tell him the truth.

That she really wanted to go parking in an old Chevy with him.

She directed her attention to the hillside. The slope was speckled with cattle, and she could see they were good strong stock. "So, you take care of the ranch?"

He nodded. "All The Boot Knockers do. And Lil."

"Oh yes. Tell me about her."

"I'm surprised you know about her. She isn't on the website or in the welcome packet, is she?"

"No, the driver mentioned her. He said this was her family's ranch she inherited and The Boot Knockers helped when she got in financial troubles."

"That's right. And at the present time, she's acting as office manager."

"Interesting. I like the thought of a woman ranchin' on her own."

His gaze was heavy and warm as he studied her.

"What?" she asked, unable to stand the pressure of those dark eyes another second. His stare made her want to take all her clothes off.

"I figured you for a strong woman right off."

"I am."

"You know what you want."

She'd taken what she'd wanted from the start—gotten her orgasm and then shut him down. Exactly what she'd set out to do.

So why wasn't she feeling that great about it? It would take some getting used to.

When applying to come to The Boot Knockers Ranch, she'd written that she was a no-nonsense woman looking for some romance in her life. That pretty much summed up the old Chevy. The new Chevy didn't want the romance, but it was Foster's job to try to melt her.

Oh yes, things were going well so far. As they headed toward a fence meandering for what seemed like miles, she knew she'd made the right decision in coming here.

Chapter Four

Foster couldn't quite puzzle this woman out. When he put his hands on her, she became a wildcat. Her responses to his kisses and touch had been so pure. But it seemed her brain got in the way and she got stiff.

He wasn't accustomed to just taking a woman without any warmup, but she'd started stripping off her cute country girl clothes and as soon as he'd seen those bare breasts, well, he'd gone a little mad. She was probably just anxious and it was a way to break the ice, to get the first encounter over with.

He still planned to wine and dine her. Then lots of sixty-ninin'. He wanted her screaming his name to the ceiling plaster, and the woman's pouty lips would look beautiful wrapped around his cock.

They strolled back to the ranch, following the fence line. In a few places, he'd stopped to inspect it for weaknesses, and she'd given her thoughts about whether or not The Boot Knockers needed to fix it.

This was better—how he liked to start things. With talk, getting to know the woman. Ninety percent of sex started in the brain, although they'd done well enough without that mental connection. Lust had driven them both, and he would have struggled to bring it to a halt, though he would have. It just wasn't his way to fuck a stranger right off.

Another couple came their way on horseback. Chevy stopped to watch them, a smile lighting her face.

So it was horses that fired her blood.

"Wanna go back and saddle up? I can grab a picnic and a bottle of wine for us."

For a second, he couldn't read her. Her eyes hazed over, and her lips parted as if she'd forgotten how to breathe. Then she gave a quick shake of her head. "No. We'll walk back and grab something to eat in the lodge."

"Okay." He could think of a dozen better places to share a meal than in the noisy hall with the other Boot Knockers and their women. He was a bit of a fish out of water with this woman.

They just needed more time together, that was all.

In the back of a truck, just them and the stars and crickets' song.

He hated a lull of silence that wasn't filled with purpose, so he said, "That guy we just passed is Trevor. He comes all the way from Canada."

"Hmm. Is he the one who specializes in oral?"

"Baby doll, that's all of us." He sent her a sideways look and managed to get a giggle out of her. "Trevor's good, though."

She looked at him in surprise. "You've seen him in action?"

"Yeah, right here." He made a motion like he was cupping a man's head at his groin.

Her jaw dropped, and she stopped walking. "What? Really?"

"Love is love, baby doll." He'd tried out a bunch of endearments on her and this one fit best so far.

"I guess you're right," she said after a minute. She set off for the cabin again.

"Does it make you hot to think of two guys together?"

"Umm." She worried her lip between her teeth, but he'd bet his shiny gold dildo that she was soaking wet and if she were sitting down, she'd be squirming the screws on the chair loose.

"Toward the end of the week, everyone gets a little friskier. Maybe you'll want to witness it for yourself and have two guys working over you."

She swung her head his direction and nearly tripped. He grabbed her elbow to right her, and his knuckles brushed the soft side of her breast. She went still. He moved in closer.

"Those lips of yours have been tormenting me for a mile and a half. Do you mind if I taste them again?"

She quivered in his hold. He applied pressure to her lower back to guide her hips into the pocket of his. She fit him perfectly.

Then he smoothed the pad of his thumb back and forth across her plush lips. Warm breath puffed against his skin. He held her gaze and dipped his head to brush one soft, chaste kiss on her mouth.

When he pulled back to stare into her eyes again, he saw that wanting. Damn, he loved putting it there. If he had his way—and he would—he'd paste that expression on her face every minute she was here.

"Let's head back to the cabin," he whispered.

She gave a dazed nod and allowed him to clasp hands with her. Within a few minutes they were at the cabin door. He took her straight to the bedroom. Without a word, he cupped her face and kissed her.

Softly at first, teasing that plump lower lip with nips and flicks of his tongue. When a quiet moan left her, he eased his hands around her shoulders. Kneading the muscles there and down to her back.

"That feels so good," she murmured, swaying in his arms.

"C'mere." He took her by the hand and led her to the bed. While they were out, housekeeping had fixed the rumpled covers. He moved some pillows and turned down the quilt. Then he reached for Chevy's buttons.

She let him strip her, which surprised him. Maybe she wasn't so tough to read, after all. With each button he unfastened, he teased the skin he exposed until he reached her navel. He circled it once with his fingertips and fluttered his fingers up to her bra.

"Let's get everything off you and then I'll show you how skilled I am in massage."

"I... am a little tense." Goosebumps prickled on her skin as he unhooked her bra.

He slipped the straps down her shoulders, rubbing those too. Her golden skin invited kisses and he couldn't wait to get his mouth all over her. But he had to take it slow or she'd bolt.

He pressed her down on the sheets and reached under her to unbutton her jeans. Pulling everything off her took seconds. When she lay face-down, nude, he gaped at the pure beauty of her. He could trace the lines of her body with his hands, lips, tongue and never get tired of her.

He scrubbed a hand over his face to find his control again and settled on the bed next to her. At first, he ran his hands over her long hair, pulling it aside. A shiver passed through her. Yessss, so responsive. He hadn't even gotten started.

"Just relax." He stroked a path from her nape to the center of her back. She undulated beneath his touch but didn't attempt to get up. He was on red alert for more of her runaway acts, but she seemed far from that now.

He worked the small muscles of her neck. At one rigid spot, she groaned. He reached over and got the massage oil from the nightstand and poured a generous dollop in his palm to heat it. When he drizzled it down

63

her spine, he had to wet his dry lips. Damn, the oil against her skin aroused the hell out of him.

He closed his eyes and let his body take over. Finding her sore spots and cajoling the muscles into relaxing. He pattered his fingers down the sides of her spine and around to her breasts, skimming as light as a butterfly's wings.

"You're so damn beautiful."

She stiffened, became a block of granite.

Shit, what had he said? She wanted romance, and him telling a woman how she looked to him always went a long way. But this woman wasn't buying it.

"You don't have to say that."

"It's true, though." He attempted to take her tension down a notch by going to the top and working his way down again. If he had to keep this up all night, he would. He only wanted to see that blissed-out look on her face again.

She didn't relax. Long minutes passed, and he could feel the tension humming just under her skin.

"Where'd you get this?" He smoothed his thumb over a small scar on her shoulder.

"The scar?"

"Yeah."

"Took a fall from a horse and hit a rock. Bled like crazy, and my momma freaked out when I limped back to the house with my shirt soaked in blood. My little sister passed out."

He gave a low chuckle. "What happened? The horse hit a hole?"

"I might have been doing something I shouldn't have."

"Oh?"

"I was trying to stand up in the saddle."

"A bit wild, are ya?"

"I was then. I wanted to be like the rodeo stars, riding the arena standing up and doing tricks."

"Did you ever try it again?"

"Try it? I mastered it."

He made a humming noise. "I'd like to see that sometime. What kind of horse?"

As she talked about her stock and ranch, she relaxed under his hands once again. Her words were coming slower, though. She was going boneless on him.

He leaned in and placed a nibble at her nape. She released a shaky sigh, and he took that as a good sign to go on. He nipped a pattern over her neck and down her shoulders. Gooseflesh rose to meet his lips.

So, she *could* be seduced — she'd just be a tough one.

She angled her head to give him better access, and he took immediate advantage. Kissing up and down, sucking on her tender flesh. If he reached under her, he'd find her nipples hard pebbles, and he wanted to flip her over and suck them. But not yet — slow.

He continued kissing her, down her spine to the crest of her buttocks. She had two small dimples at the small of her back, and he lapped at them for long seconds before drawing a line to the top of her crack.

She gasped.

"Shhh." By the end of the week, he'd explore her everywhere, but he didn't want to frighten her by going too fast. He gently rolled her onto her back.

Her eyes glowed up at him, and he couldn't resist brushing her hair off her forehead and leaning in to claim her lips. A soft kiss that held so much promise for a glorious night.

He moved down her body, kissing and tasting her until he reached the small strip of curls pointing toward her wet pussy. Her outer lips glistened with juices.

Juices he was going to lick up.

He sprawled between her legs and looped her legs over his shoulders.

A quiet moan broke from her, and he answered with a hungry rumble. As he sank his tongue between her slick folds, it became a growl. She cried out, pushing into his mouth. He sucked at her clit until it strained under his lips. Then he swirled his tongue down to her opening.

They shared a rough noise, and he felt her stop breathing. In five more passes of his tongue, she was grabbing at his hair, tugging him upward.

It took him less than thirty seconds to strip his clothes off and don a condom.

"Foster," she whispered, her lips swollen and her cheeks flushed with color.

He hovered over her, his cock head pointed to her liquid heat like an arrow on a compass. Without hesitation, he entered her in one slow, slippery, gut-clenching glide.

As he bottomed out inside her, he watched her eyes haze with a new light.

Confusion.

She wasn't certain of her own reaction to him, and he needed to change that. By the time she left his bed, she'd be the confident sex-kitten she was born to be.

He poured himself into a kiss. Fuck, he wanted her like no other. His drive to taste, explore, conquer... He couldn't get enough. And all those little moans she made were making him crazy.

Halfway through, he realized he was bending his own mind in the process.

He sank into her. Sank in again. She gripped him with her inner walls like they'd done this a thousand times. When he cupped her ass and jerked her up to meet his thrusts, he pushed half an inch deeper.

"Oh God," she cried out, scrabbling at his shoulders with her blunt nails.

"You're hugging me so damn tight. Fuck, baby doll."

She issued a rough moan that sliced through him. In a blink, he was on the verge of blowing.

Not yet. Fuck, not yet. Make it good for —

She clamped around him, and each rhythmic pulsation shot through the nerves of his cock. He pushed deep and dragged her up into his kiss as he exploded in ecstasy.

* * * * *

Holy Hades on toast, this man was great in the sack. Her cry echoed in the room, mixing with his harsh breathing.

And they'd almost come at the same time. Like, within a second of each other. Maybe even a nanosecond. That was new for her, something you didn't achieve with partners you've been with for years.

Oh. Crap.

She was doing it again, wasn't she? Romanticizing their connection, when all they had was a client/Boot Knocker relationship. She wiggled, and he looked down at her with that lazy crooked grin that said he knew he'd blown her mind.

Triple damn. She was frazzled, rattled and more freakin' satisfied than she'd ever been.

Maybe she was a hopeless case. She'd never stop falling for assholes, and she was sure this was no different, only that she was paying him to be nice.

Before she could tell him to get out of bed, he did a pushup over her and kissed her. Long, deep, until her toes curled against his strong calves.

A dark shiver ruffled through her senses, and she felt that old euphoria rising up. The floating feeling that happened after she'd had great sex with a great man. Or at least one she thought was great.

"Um... can you get up?" She pushed against his shoulders to lever him away.

"Sorry, am I crushing you, baby doll?"

Why did he have to call her that? It was cute and sweet wrapped up in three small syllables. She liked it far too much, mostly because it was new to her. The guys from her past always seemed to call her sweetie or honey. There'd been one honey bunch in there, which had made her feel like he was a relative. Good thing they'd broken up a few days later.

Foster rolled off but didn't budge from his position on the mattress. He was stretched out, his big body at ease, his cock shrinking inside the used condom. He didn't seem in any rush to leave.

She dragged in a deep breath. She was no good at dumping people. She was always on the receiving end of that conversation. But she was here to take the upper hand.

She sat up and yanked the quilt off the bed, wrapping up in it.

His eyes crinkled at the corners with a smile. "Where ya goin'? No need to be so modest. I've seen all of ya."

"I…" Could she speak her mind? Yes, she could. "Can you just leave?"

She saw her words struck him hard. He jerked his chin back as if she'd punched him. Then he swung his legs over the edge of the bed. "You want me to leave?"

"Y-yes."

"But… why? Did I do something wrong, baby doll? I thought you were satisfied. I felt you—"

Don't remind me or I'll never send you away.

He got up and circled the bed to where she stood. If she tried to back up in the quilt, she'd trip. She stood her ground and stared him in the eyes.

"I'm going to pack," she said.

He stopped in his tracks, part sexy male and part confused boy. He scratched his jaw, and a rasping noise made her squeeze her thighs together. "You haven't *un*packed, Chevy. Do you plan on leaving?"

"Yes, I made a mistake. This place isn't for me." She hadn't known that was her decision until the words burst from her. Looking at the hurt cross his face made her want to eat them all again, though. He really had done a good job—great, in fact. He was so good at his work that she realized she didn't have a prayer of resisting his charms. She'd fall for them over and over. She needed someone less skilled to practice being a hard-ass on.

He reached for her, but she edged back, somehow managing to remain upright.

He shoved his fingers through his dark hair, sending it into spikes. Her instinct was to shove off the blanket and smooth those strands into place and kiss away the crease between his brow she'd put there.

But that was the old Chevy.

"If we went too fast, I'm deeply sorry, Chevy. Please forgive me. Say the word and I won't touch you again. Just stay on the ranch and enjoy some rest. There's lots to do around here. You can even help me work if you'd like. Might be good to see what a bigger operation does, get some ideas for when you go home."

She faltered at his words. Could she really just spend the rest of the week in his presence without giving in to his wiles? It would be good practice. And she *had* paid a huge sum of money for this trip. She could have taken several tropical vacations for one week with a Boot Knocker in Montana.

She pushed out a breath through her nose, undecided.

He searched her gaze, leaving her feeling exposed, and she didn't like it.

She raised her jaw a notch. "All right, but just to see the ranch."

"Good. Now come lie down with me. As friends." His eyes twinkled.

Her heart flipped and sped off at a faster gallop. Shit, she was far from cured. If she ever could be. She was a terminal romantic.

"Or we can sit on the sofa." He waved to the other room and the spaces they hadn't even used yet.

She looked at the inviting bed and the hunky man she wanted standing so close to it. If only she could just enjoy a fantastic lover for the next few days without all the baggage.

She could try.

"The bed looks better than the sofa."

"There's a reason for that. We're supposed to keep you in bed."

She blinked. *Ouch.*

She was just a job to him.

How stupid. Even when she believed she wasn't falling for it, she was. Already had. Now she remembered why she was here.

* * * * *

Foster relished the burn of his muscles as he shoveled. The scrape of the metal against earth and rock gave him deep satisfaction, which centered him right now.

After falling asleep in the same bed, with Chevy curled away from him, he'd woken with her in his arms. He'd watched the sunrise creep over her beautiful face and wondered what the hell he was doing wrong with her.

She'd come here looking to be romanced, and at times he saw a crack in her shell, but then she'd steel herself and reject everything he said and did.

He shook his head. He didn't get it. In his life, he hadn't failed at many things, but the hollow feeling he got when he saw that unhappiness in Chevy's eyes made him think he was failing now.

"Whoa, Fos. You're not trying kill the earth, are you?" Shayne looked up from his own post hole he was digging.

Foster realized he was stabbing the edges of his own hole. "Guess I got carried away."

"What's up with you? You're not your usual happy-go-lucky self."

Foster pressed his lips into a firm line and considered telling his buddy everything. Instead, he asked Shayne a question. "How're things with your new woman?"

Shayne waggled his brows. "Slow starter, but once she warms up, we need a fire extinguisher." He grabbed his crotch.

Foster gave a half-smile. "Why's she here?" Sometimes they bounced ideas off each other if they were having trouble with a certain woman. But Foster had never had that issue. In real life or on The Boot Knockers Ranch.

"She's had some boyfriends telling her she's bad in bed. I say they were just doing it wrong. Think I convinced her too. Now we have all week to fuck like bunnies."

Staring at the hole for a moment, Foster didn't speak.

"You having some trouble up in Cabin 3?"

"Not exactly."

"But things aren't going the way you want them to, right?"

"You got it."

"Have you tried your signature bubble bath move?"

He shook his head. "She's only been here a day."

"But you kept her up all night fucking her." Shayne started on his hole again. Thankfully, he was looking at the ground instead of Foster and didn't see him wince.

When he didn't respond, Shayne looked up. "Fos?"

"Yeah, it's all good," he said hastily and started digging.

Chevy had actually been the one to spot the two sections of fencing that were weak during her tour of the ranch. He'd been too busy looking at her. Something about the lines of her face felt familiar. Like he'd touched them before, followed them with his fingers and lips. He hadn't been able to figure out why a woman like her hadn't found a man with enough game to satisfy her yet.

But when he gave her sweet words, she shot him down. And after sex, she'd bounced out of bed without a backward glance, as cold as ice.

Maybe he should talk to Lil, get Chevy's file from her. He must be missing something, like she had some other hang-ups and wasn't only looking for a romantic weekend with a cowboy who was damn good at his job.

The past twenty-four hours had him questioning his skill, though.

He got the hole to the depth needed to set the new post. They were sister-ing two posts together connected by a strong cross brace to shore up the fence. Not exactly a usual way of doing things, but he thought the outcome would do well.

As they worked, Shayne talked about the chores Lil had cornered him about and told him to get done. Foster listened but didn't add much. When they finished, he glanced at the sky to gauge the time, but it was overcast today.

"It's nine-thirty. Still time for breakfast. I don't know about you, but I'm cleaning up and getting my girl out of bed for some of Cook's pancakes and homemade sausage. Or maybe I'll just climb in bed with her."

"Who needs food?" Foster threw him a grin as he rested the shovel over his shoulder and headed down the hill toward the lodge. With each step, he thought of how to give Chevy what she needed. Several screaming orgasms didn't seem to make her happy. Afterward, she was more troubled than before.

Without knowing more about her, it was difficult to know how to fix it.

He bypassed the cabins and went straight to the office, leaving his shovel outside. Lil was seated behind the desk, looking less harried than she had been lately.

"You must be getting the feel of things around here," he said as he entered.

"Nope. Hate this job with a burning passion. Hugh assures me I'll have a replacement in another week or so. They interviewed some good candidates by phone and just need to do some background checks."

"That's good. Real good."

She narrowed her gaze at him. "Why are you here? Shouldn't you be working on that fence?"

"Done. Shayne and I just finished. Your cattle are safe."

"Good. And thank you," she added.

"Sure. Now I can use a favor."

"Oh no. Tell me you aren't out of the extra-extra-large condoms, because I don't believe you've used even one of that size unless you're putting more than one dick in it."

He chuckled. "That's a common occurrence around here."

"You're joking." Her face was blank.

"Yeah, I'm just messin' with ya. I need to see my client's file."

"You've seen it."

He eyed her. "The whole file." There was a section held back from the Boot Knockers, and he was certain it harbored the information he needed to crack Chevy.

Lil chewed her lower lip. He'd think it was cute if he hadn't seen Chevy biting hers and found it much cuter. "I'm not supposed to. It's against the rules."

"Since when do you follow rules?"

She blinked at him. "You're right. I don't." She swiveled in her chair to the wall of files behind her. She searched through them and plucked one free. Holding it against her chest, she said, "I'll let you see if you promise not to tell anyone. If word gets out, I'll be fired."

At that, he laughed. "You can't be fired. You're just filling in."

She smacked her palm off her forehead. "God, I'm so screwed up working in here. I've never spent so much time indoors since I was in the womb. I'm losing it, Foster."

He reached for the file, and she handed it to him. "We'll get you out of here soon. If Hugh doesn't come through, we can take turns in the office on our off weeks."

"Damn, why didn't I think to suggest that when Hugh and Riggs foisted this godawful job on me? Oh yeah." She turned a glare on him. "Somebody was on their side, using his skills to back them up and talk me into it."

He flipped open the file, suddenly absorbed by the photo of Chevy in the upper corner. The selfie was the same one he'd seen before she'd come to the ranch, but her beauty fist-punched him.

"Why don't you head on outside and get some fresh air, Lil? I'll put this back when I'm done."

She was out of the seat before he'd finished the sentence. He leaned against the desk and read through Chevy's information. Private info they weren't allowed to see, such as address and social media. The ranch did thorough checks on each woman before she came here to ensure she was of sound mind. They didn't need trouble, and on paper, Chevy looked as normal as they came.

A few pages in, he stopped. There was a short essay written by Chevy about why she thought The Boot Knockers Ranch would benefit her.

I'd love to feel special, to have a man dote on me and show me real romance.

That sentence didn't seem to fit her. In fact, he wondered if she'd even written it.

He leafed through the final pages, which told him nothing, and then he returned the file to the shelf, probably in the wrong spot, but hell, he was no office manager. He went outside. Lil was nowhere in sight.

He headed to the cabin, but it was empty. Dang, he was seriously fucking this up. Chevy wasn't supposed to wander the ranch alone. He strode back to the lodge and spotted her straightaway in the dining hall. Her back was to him as she moved through the buffet.

He pushed out a rush of air. She looked damn fine in a pair of skinny jeans and boots. Her red plaid top skimmed the curves of her torso and waist and her hair was in a thick braid over one shoulder.

Over the years, he'd seen a lot of women, but this little country girl revved his engine big time.

He strode up to her and hovered close to her ear. "You're looking stunning this morning, baby doll."

She released a shivery sigh and then tensed and used some tongs to grab a few fat strawberries. She dropped them onto her plate like they'd done her real harm.

Crap, so she was still as confusing today as yesterday. He took the plate from her and balanced it on one palm while he closed his fingers around hers. Holding her gaze, he brought her knuckles to his lips.

"You don't have to do that, you know." Her expression was wary.

"What?"

"Pretend you're interested. I thought we hashed this out last night."

He continued to hold her hand. "What if I'm not pretending? Is it so hard to believe you have merits that make a man want to be with you?"

She eyed him, her lips set in a straight line.

"Baby doll, I can see you've got something to say. Might as well get it off your chest." He took the liberty of moving down the buffet line and adding several homemade sausage patties to her plate, as well as some ripe melon. He had no idea if she liked it or not, but he wanted to taste it on her lips.

She didn't say anything, only followed him to a table. He waited for her to sit before placing the plate before her, along with silverware. He went back to the buffet to grab his own plate and some OJ for them. When he returned, she was staring at her food but not eating.

"Your food isn't giving you any answers, I reckon." He sank down beside her and scooted as close as he dared without triggering her to get up and leave.

"No," she said unhappily.

"You know I'm here to help you, right? Whatever reason you came doesn't matter. I'm here to work through it with you."

She raised her gaze to his, and he saw the warm depths shining with hesitation.

He picked up his knife and fork, tines down, and dug into his sausage.

She opened her mouth and he tried to focus on his food rather than center his attention on her. Though that's what he wanted to do. Everything about her was going against his instincts. But if it helped her, that was all that mattered.

In a halting voice, she said, "I've... fallen for some dumbasses in my day."

Shayne popped his head over her shoulder, making her jump. "Foster's far from a regular dumbass. He's got what? Four college degrees?"

"Five," Foster said with his mouth full.

Her eyes popped out. "Seriously?"

He gave her a smile and a small shrug. "What do degrees matter when you've got all this going on?" He waved a hand over his body.

She giggled and picked up her fork... stabbed a piece of sausage and popped it into her mouth. "I see what you mean."

Chapter Five

Watching a cowboy like Foster work around the ranch was enough to make any girl sit up and take notice. Or beg. He was as strong and tough as he was graceful and agile. He climbed the ladder to the hayloft in five seconds flat and hung by one arm like a monkey just to make her cover her eyes in worry.

Then he shimmied down, leaping the last eight feet to land next to her.

"Show-off," she said.

"Ain't gonna apologize for it."

She considered him. "You really have that many degrees?"

"It's been coming up a lot lately. I'm wondering why it's suddenly so important. I'm still plain old Foster."

He was anything but plain old. He was obviously smart and knew his way around a ranch.

And around her body.

"Keep eyeing me that way, baby doll, and I'll forget my promises to keep my hands off you."

She stared at his eyelids drooping over his smoldering eyes and appreciated how one look could make her body stir. Okay, who was she kidding? She was fully aroused. If he slid into her now, he'd find her soaking. Her nipples throbbed dully and she wished she could strip and guide them to his hard lips.

"Chevy." His voice came out as a warning. He took a step toward her.

Maybe she should go for it. Why not? It could just be gratuitous, hip-grinding, dirty sex. Every time he opened his mouth to schmooze her, she could cut him off with a kiss.

He gazed into her eyes, waiting to see what she'd do.

She'd come here to learn how to move on, and throwing herself at a man was the old Chevy.

But rolling in the hay was out of the norm. Even the vet hadn't wooed her with sex in the barn.

She moved toward Foster. His eyes widened and then a crooked smile of appreciation quirked his lips. She slipped her arms around his neck and leaned close to whisper in his ear.

"I've never been fucked in the hay."

He didn't hesitate to snap his arms around her waist and whirl her toward the nearest hay bale. He set her down hard, and she stifled a giggle as he spun her to bend over the hay. Before she could even glance back at him to see what he intended to do, he smacked her ass.

"Wicked woman, teasing a hardworking man like me. Distracting me from my job."

"I thought I *was* your job."

"Not anymore. You fired me from it, remember?"

He sort of fired himself, but she didn't say anything because he grabbed her hips and yanked her back against his erection. Hard as steel, locked and loaded. He was rock to her roll.

Dammit, she'd been crazy to come here, but she wasn't going to stop him now—not when she was burning for him.

She arched her back, rubbing her ass against him. He growled against her neck. "You're playing with wildfire."

"Interesting you wouldn't just say fire."

He flicked his tongue over her throat, shooting pangs of need between her thighs.

"Fire's what you've got in a circle of rocks. Harnessed. Controlled."

Goosebumps broke out on her skin, and her nipples peaked so tightly, she moaned.

He reached under her top, moving rough hands against her soft abs and up to cup her breasts through her bra. With a precision most men didn't have, Foster pinched her nipples.

Perfectly hard.

She hummed her pleasure.

"Still want to dance in the flames, baby doll?"

"Oh God, yes."

She didn't need to utter another word. He shoved her bra up and her pants down. He grazed her outer buttocks with his palm before she heard the telltale *clink* of his belt buckle. Holding her breath in anticipation, she drank in the moment.

Hay, sunlight, dust swirling in the air. Behind her, a rock-solid man who was about to bend her over the hay bale and blow her mind.

Her breath rushed out when she saw the condom wrapper flutter to the barn floor by her foot. Two seconds didn't pass before Foster was with her — inside her.

She gulped back a cry of bliss as his thick head stroked her innermost walls. "It's sooo deep."

"That's the angle. Fuck!" He sank to the base, and his balls slapped her pussy.

She ground against him, and he drove his cock deeper.

"Oh yeahhh." He grunted.

She loved pulling all these noises and harsh words from him. It turned her on like nothing else. And she felt the clenching of his fingers in her hips and heard his labored breathing. He wasn't putting on an act to woo her. He wanted to fuck her.

Suddenly, she realized she *could* go on here at the ranch and just make this about sex and relaxation. She didn't need to tie herself emotionally to this man.

He cupped her jaw and twisted her head to kiss her. The instant he sank his tongue into her mouth, the fever inside her grew hotter. She was so close, so…

Her orgasm hit out of nowhere. She clamped around his shaft, pulling a groan from him. Stars blinded her, and she hardly had any notion of his hips churning as he pounded a fast and furious pace.

Only his rough breath washing over her ear roused her from her slumping position over the hay. The hot spill of his cum warmed her through the condom, and she let her eyes slip shut. He cradled her against his chest as the final twitches of her release faded.

"Damn." He turned his lips to her throat and placed small licks and kisses that extended her aftershocks. Her pussy tightened around him again, and he groaned.

"You make a lot of noise," she teased, throwing a glance over her shoulder.

His rumble of amusement vibrated through her spine and warmed her.

He trailed his nose up to her ear. When he sank his teeth into her lobe, she slapped at him. He laughed again. "What can I say about the noises? You bring them out of me, baby doll." He moved his hips, sliding his still engorged cock through her walls and free of her body.

She squeezed on the emptiness, but he turned her gently into his arms, cupped her nape and kissed her.

This time, she didn't let herself get carried away by the kiss. She focused on the pleasure he'd given her… and the fun too. "I've never had sex in the barn before."

He arched a brow at her, which only made him look more wicked. "Country girl like you?"

"Yep. I've been in beds piled with pillows and five-star hotel suites."

"Time to get down and dirty then." He flashed a grin, teeth white in his tanned face and almost wolfish.

Oh yes, she'd be getting down and dirty with this man over and over again this week. It might have taken her a little while to understand what she wanted from this Boot Knocker, but now she was ready to play hard.

She wouldn't look at his dark eyes and pretend she saw more there. And he could shove his candlelight dinners where the sun didn't shine. She'd take the fun romps over those awful words—making love—any day.

* * * * *

Foster kept throwing looks at Chevy as she galloped beside him. The wind whipped her hair on her spine. It must be tangled. Maybe she'd let him brush it for her tonight.

In the barn, after they'd pulled their clothing into order, she'd walked away as if he hadn't just given her the time of her life. If he had less of an ego, her nonchalance would start to wear on him.

He'd seen the glint in her eye that said she'd enjoyed their play, and he kept that in mind as she'd tried to ignore him.

He'd had plenty of country girls in his youth, but none like Chevy. She knew her way around cattle and was full of enthusiasm for everything he showed her on the ranch.

She also kept him coming back for more. Maybe it was the game of cat and mouse that was making him spin donuts, but he wanted her bad.

She spurred her horse faster. He did the same, coming beside her. They rode flat-out for several minutes before slowing. Bringing the horses to a trot, she said, "That felt good. This horse handles almost the same as my own."

"He knows a good rider when he sees it."

"Flattery will get you nowhere."

In this case, he believed her.

He lifted his jaw toward her hands. "Your grip's off."

Annoyance flashed in her deep brown eyes. "You're crazy."

He showed how he gripped the reins.

She leaned over to get a better look. "You have the snaffle rein between the middle and ring finger and the curb rein between your ring and pinky finger."

"Yeah, gives more precise commands."

"I do fine in the traditional two-and-two method. Did you see me struggling?" Her face flushed red.

He watched the color rise in the apples of her cheeks and let a crooked smile quirk his mouth. "No. I just wanted to fuck with you and see you get mad."

She sputtered. "Why would you want to do that?"

"You're cute when you're angry. C'mon. Yah!" He set his horse to a run, and she followed, zigzagging across the fields until they reached a copse of trees. He reined up and she did the same.

"You're a jerk, ya know."

"I know." He swung out of the saddle and set his horse loose to graze on the sweet grasses. Foster twisted off one stem and stuck it between his teeth to chew on.

Chevy dismounted too and her horse joined his in foraging for a snack. "Why are we here?"

"Pretty place to stop, ain't it?"

She blinked at him.

"Say what's on your mind, baby doll. I can see you're gnawing on something."

She cocked her head. "How does a man as educated as you use bad grammar?"

"I can use good grammar if I choose." He adopted a stuffy accent. He gave her another crooked smile and she returned it. "It's in the genes, I guess. My dad only has an eighth-grade education. He's done fine for himself."

"Really?"

He walked into the cove of trees. Years of fallen leaves had provided a soft cushion on the ground, and he took a seat in the shade, his back against a trunk. He patted the ground next to him.

She came reluctantly, as if she sensed a trick. But by now he'd caught on that she didn't like the traditional ways of romance. "C'mon, Chevy. I'm not going to whip out a bunch of candles and light them for a romantic interlude."

She giggled. "I thought you carried them with you everywhere, since it's your nickname."

94

"Common misconception." He reached into his shirt pocket and came out with a paper bag folded into a hard rectangle. As he opened it, she watched with wide eyes. He withdrew a stick of homemade beef jerky that Cook had recently spiced and dried.

He held it out to her, and Chevy took it and plopped down beside him. He made room so she could lean on the tree too. The warmth of her body seeped through his jeans and shirt sleeve, a sensation he liked. A lot.

"Tell me about your dad." She bit off a chunk of jerky. "Mm, this is good."

"The best." He took the grass from his mouth and replaced it with jerky. After he'd chewed and swallowed, he said, "My dad's parents died young in a car crash, and he was on his own."

"No family?"

"Not exactly. Just family who didn't want him. So he made his own way, but he was in and out of boys' homes and a few foster homes before he ran off. He's worked hard all his life to provide for my mother, me and my two brothers."

"That's amazing. What's he do?"

"Construction. Learned the trade by apprenticing with a few builders before he was even eighteen, learned everything he needed to know. Eventually he started getting hired for odd jobs, and he just turned it into a career."

"And he put you through college."

"I went on a scholarship, the first time." He chewed off more beef jerky. The wind whispered through the trees, bringing the fresh scents of growing things. And Chevy. Her vanilla-coconut body wash was driving him to distraction.

"That's fantastic."

He nodded. "Pretty lucky. Then I got the learnin' bug and couldn't stop until I had several degrees." He looked at her. Dang, she was adorable when she chewed. He was aroused just sitting here watching her eat.

"Impressive." Her smile was true.

He lowered his strip of jerky. "I'll show you somethin' impressive."

She released a huff of laughter. "I believe you showed me once today."

"Yeah, but there's more." He caught her wrist and brought her hand to his fly.

Her eyes widened. "Hmm. *Very* impressive, I'd say."

"Watch it or it'll all go to my head." He flattened her hand over his bulging cock head.

Suddenly, her jerky went flying into the leafy floor and she threw herself at him. He yanked her across his lap in a straddle. When she leaned in to kiss him, their hats tumbled off.

Things heated up. He crushed his lips to hers, and she slipped her tongue into his mouth to dance across his own. They roughly removed each other's clothes.

That was how he fucked Chevy in his favorite spot on the ranch.

Chapter Six

Chevy froze as she heard the water hitting the bathtub. The big, deep bathtub large enough for two people.

She gripped the stem of her glass of red wine, her mind working through how to get out of this situation. She had managed not to entangle her emotions in the grove of trees with Foster, but now that she heard that bathtub filling, she got that familiar high feeling that accompanied being wooed.

The tripping of her pulse, the flutter in her chest... Yep, signs of falling.

Falling flat into a pile of bullshit.

She would not drift to the bathroom door and peek in. Nope, she was sitting right here and sipping her wine. In a little while, she'd go to the hall for dinner.

There was a knock at the front door, and she looked up, startled. Who would be coming to the cabin? She could just ignore it, pretend she hadn't heard the visitor. They'd understand because how often were the inhabitants of the cabins indisposed?

Another tap on the door. She set down her goblet with a sigh and went for the door. She opened it to find a sexy cowboy on the doorstep. He was holding a box. *Well, hello. Whatever you're selling, I'm buying.*

He offered her a grin that would make any woman pick her tongue up off the floor. Then he tipped his hat.

Oh lawdy, these Boot Knockers are trying to kill me.

She'd need to wipe the drool off her face if he didn't hurry up and tell her why he was here.

"Howdy, miss. Name's Wyoming. Foster asked me to swing by and bring these." He extended the box, plain brown wrapped in a red satin ribbon.

"Oh. Thank you."

Foster's heat enveloped her back as he looked around her. Wyoming's smile grew lazier, sultrier. Chevy twisted to see Foster grinning at the man. Damn, was Wyoming here for some other reason?

The thought seemed connected directly to her clit, and she felt a tug of arousal.

Foster took the box. "Thanks for bringing this up, Wyoming. You playing messenger for Lil now?"

"Here and there. Mostly she's got me busting my balls on the ranch—" He stopped and fingered the brim of his hat. "Sorry for the coarse language, miss."

Chevy hid a smile behind her hand. "It's fine."

Foster wrapped his fingers around the long braid running down her back as he casually slumped against the doorframe to speak with his friend. She didn't know how to feel about the casual touch, because it felt intimate beyond words. In the back of the cabin, the water still filled the tub. She'd had no intention of being lured into that hot water, probably filled with bubble bath and maybe even floating flower petals. But now she couldn't shake the idea of sinking into the water and leaning back against Foster.

"Lil is determined to get that new cattle shelter up by the end of the week. But we need more manpower if that's going to happen."

"Maybe we can bring all the ladies with us. Let 'em watch us sweat." Foster dropped Chevy a wink. Warmth bloomed behind her breasts in a spot she could not—would not—recognize as being her heart.

Freakin' hell on a cracker. She wasn't falling for this shit.

She pulled away from him and went back to pick up her glass. She downed the wine in one gulp while listening to the water burble and the men's voices as they ended their conversation.

Foster closed the door. She heard his footsteps but wasn't going to turn and look into his eyes. He'd control her if she did, and she wasn't going there. No way.

She felt him approach, too aware of the heat coming off his body. She wanted to turn into his arms, let him pick her up and carry her to bed.

The box appeared under her nose, that satin ribbon teasing her to tug it off.

"What's this?" she asked.

"Open it." He came around to stand before her. Sculpted muscles in worn jeans and a black T-shirt. Could he get any sexier? He could wear a 1970s leisure suit and still look hot as hell.

He stepped in closer. He wasn't wearing a hat and it would be so easy to sink her fingers into his thick hair.

"Is the water going to overflow?" she asked to cover her distraction.

"Not likely. That's a deep tub. But why don't you take your gift into the bathroom and see for yourself?" He gave her a gentle push in the direction. Too stunned to think up some snarky response, she went.

The scent of lavender hit her senses, and her hair started to curl at the steam in the air. Foster closed the door behind her, and she blinked in surprise. He hadn't tried to come in with her. Maybe he was listening to her wishes not to be charmed, pampering her but not making it a couple's thing.

She glanced at the tub. The water was rising—and it was bright purple. As bright as a little girl's favorite crayon. She laughed. This was far from the bubble bath and rose petals she'd pictured.

She sat on the granite ledge and rested the box on her knees. As the water continued to rise, she removed the ribbon. Hesitating for a moment. What if she saw jewelry?

She'd open the door and throw it in his face, that's what. She had a whole jewelry box full of castoffs, gifts from men who had eventually revealed their true selves.

With a determined deep breath, she pulled off the lid.

She stared at the fat wad of cotton and what rested on it. Not diamonds or gems, but leather.

A horse halter, triple-stitched with hand-rubbed edges. She picked it up and turned it over and over, examining the adjustable crown and solid brass hardware.

Her throat closed off.

Dammit. Damn Foster. He'd sunk his hooks into her with the only gift from a man she'd actually accept. Her mare would appreciate the comfort of this new halter.

Setting the box aside, she took off her clothes and sank into the shimmering purple water. As she rested her head against the floating bath pillow, she considered the man who'd done these things for her.

Nice try, but she saw through his game. They may be slightly off-beat—the purple water and the halter—but they were the same methods used by men everywhere since the beginning of time. Except back in the day, Moses had probably given his woman a goat lead and taken her to the nearest spring to cool off.

The longer she sat there in the tub of violet water, the more agitated she became. In a splash, she burst to her feet, dripping and mad. She grabbed a towel and hastily wrapped it around herself.

When she threw open the bathroom door, Foster was there. His dark eyes glowed with something that made her breath hitch. Without a word, he strode to her and ripped off her towel.

* * * * *

He had no idea what he was doing. All he knew was he had to put his hands on Chevy — now. Running on pure instinct, he picked her up, wet, naked and squirming, and threw her over his shoulder.

"What are you doing? Let me down!" She kicked her heels, which only made him hotter for her. He loved a sassy woman, and she was that and more.

On his way to the bed, he grabbed the bottle of wine she'd left there.

She gave a hard kick, and he let her go, as she asked. She tumbled onto the mattress, hair in her face. She sputtered and brushed it aside to reveal two eyes, bright with fury. Her lips pursed, but he knew she wouldn't hold back her words for long.

He started counting. Three, two…

She shoved onto her elbows, which only made her breasts bounce and his cock harder. "You can't just toss me around."

"Already did." He uncorked the bottle and upended it on her stomach. Red wine ran off her skin, pooling in her navel and the hollows of her hips.

"What the?" She started to move but he dipped his head to the wine. He ran his tongue through the bright notes of Muscat grapes. Across her lower belly, slurping at her navel.

She went still as he zigzagged his tongue lower, lower still. Wine flowed in a thin stream between her thighs, and he followed it like an explorer in the New World. Using the point of his tongue, he found his treasure.

Her head dropped back, and she sucked in a harsh gasp. He licked at her clit, and she parted her thighs for him.

"Mmm. Delicious." He flashed a look at her face, made more beautiful by bliss, and opened his mouth over her pussy. Sucking, licking, teasing. He kept her anchored under him with one hand and reached out for the bottle with the other.

When he dribbled more wine on her skin, she sucked back a cry. Fisted the sheets.

Wine streamed down her body into his open mouth. He sank his alcohol and pussy-wet tongue into her tight entrance. Her inner muscles clutched at him, but he planned to tease her a hell of a long time before giving her release. She had to realize loving was about much more than empty promises, shallow words and vanilla sex.

When she left here, he wanted her to remember this moment. Coming fresh from the purple bath smelling of lavender and him drinking wine off her perfect body.

Getting drunk on her.

He closed his eyes, lapping along her seam, listening to only her soft cries and his own heartbeat. Something about her was tearing at him. He wanted to get closer and closer.

He lifted his head and kissed along her inner thigh up to her knee. She grabbed him by the hair and dragged him back to her pussy. Rumbling laughter, he did the bidding of his sweet, wine-drenched goddess and worshipped her the way she demanded.

He teased her with his fingertips, circling her opening while sucking at her clit. When he swirled his finger downward over her tight pucker, she cried out.

So his sexy, sassy cowgirl liked being touched there. He pushed her thighs up and back, rolling her up to meet his tongue. As he licked at her most forbidden spot, he felt her start to shake. For long minutes, he worked over her, until he felt the first strong pulsations that heralded she was about to come.

He pushed two fingers deep into her pussy and covered her clit with strong pulls of his mouth. Her moans grew louder until she was screaming with each stroke of his fingers. When she came, it was going to be huge. She was strung so tight, and he was aching hard for her.

"Oh my God. Foster!"

He kept up his torment. She bucked her hips. He finger-fucked her more shallowly, pressing on her G-spot as he did. She swelled against him.

They were both wound so tight, one or both were going to blow soon or the world would implode. He slowed his movements. She peaked and cried out.

* * * * *

What was this man doing to her? Her brain wasn't even connected to her body — she was floating on a haze of sexual ecstasy. Each contraction of her pussy sent shockwaves through her system. She fisted the sheets, threw back her head and screamed.

He slowed his tongue and glided his fingers out of her. Then he hovered over her, his yummy lips inches away. When he kissed her, he tasted of alcohol and her.

A sudden splash of wine hit the corner of her mouth, and she jumped. The liquid ran off her. They were going to leave these sheets stained beyond repair, but he didn't seem to care. Leaning back, he let a fat drop of wine hit her lips. She licked them clean, and he did too, his warm, wet mouth exciting her all over again.

He fed her more wine, and passion flowed. She reached for him, finding him hard and throbbing in her palm. As she closed her fist around his length and stroked him, his eyes darkened.

Against her mouth, he groaned. "Your hand feels so fucking good."

Encouraged to do more, she leaned up and bit his nipple while jacking his cock. It tightened in her mouth, and she flicked her tongue over it.

No man had ever felt this good to her. She wanted to give him the same pleasure she'd known moments before. She released him and slithered down his body. He hovered over her, braced on strong arms, his cock jutting toward her lips.

She mouthed his straining head, tasting his salty pre-cum and let out a moan of her own. Then she parted her lips and enveloped him. Right to the root.

He jerked his hips, sinking deeper into her throat. She closed her eyes and reveled in his scents and the feel of him, so worked up because of her. It was a high she hadn't known in a long time, and even that had never been this euphoric.

She threw herself into making Foster feel good. Somehow it didn't matter who'd come before her—she just wanted to be remembered for blowing his mind.

She ran her tongue up and down the underside of his shaft, and he stiffened. The muscles tightened along his back, and she knew he was close.

With a harsh groan, he rolled off her and dragged her up to his lips. She kissed him for a long time. Suckling kisses that were in no hurry. They were tailgate-down, under-the-moonlight kisses. She wouldn't mind doing that either.

He cupped the back of her head, eyes looming close. "Get the condom."

She leaned over and reached into the drawer that was amply stocked with everything and anything they'd need. There was even a little silver bullet vibe she might have him try out on her later.

With a wicked grin, she opened the packet and fitted it to the tip of his erection. She started to smooth it over his girth, but he stilled her hand, clamping it under his. "Let me do it," he said roughly. A quick jerk of his wrist and it was in place. Then he was pulling her into the saddle, straddling him.

"Giddyap, cowgirl." His eyes twinkled, but she saw it was an effort for him to not move.

She could torture him for a long time, as he had her. But his throbbing cock beckoned to her, and she couldn't stop herself from easing over him. As he filled her, stretched her, she let out a raspy sigh.

He gripped her backside. "Ready to ride?"

"Ready to fly," she said.

He grinned and drew her down on top of him. He'd barely seated himself fully inside her when she pushed off again. He pulled her back down. Five times, ten. A push and pull, a battle of forces that would give them both the end they craved.

Her pussy was so wet, his cock so hard. Together, they made a great team.

He crushed his lips to hers in a primal, tongue-winding kiss until she couldn't take it anymore. She shattered with a cry. He followed seconds after, and they tumbled into the sheets, kissing, wound around each other.

* * * * *

Foster stood at the side of the bed. He leaned over his lover and stamped a kiss to her lips.

"Where are you going?" She leaned on one elbow to look at him. She wished she'd gotten out of bed first—it made her seem needy and not at all like the woman who was determined to keep him at arm's length.

"Problem on the ranch. Gotta take care of this." He eyed her for a second. "Come with me."

The way he said it—a request instead of a question—got her on her feet.

He stood back to appraise her curves even as he reached for his jeans. She reached for hers too, watching him back. He was a damn fine man, and she'd had the sex of a lifetime with him. She also liked that he was taking care of the ranch duties.

"What's going on?" she asked, hooking her bra.

He gaped at her for a moment as if words failed him. She ducked her head to hide a grin. It made her feel strong and sexy to be wanted by a man like Foster. And stronger and sexier that she knew she could walk away from him at the end of the week without regrets. If she could channel this into her everyday life, then she'd broken her cycle.

"Elk on the ranch."

She paused. "Elk?"

"Yeah, come up from the lower lands for summer grazing. Cooler up here. But we don't

112

want them driving our cattle off and mowing off all the best grazing land."

"I've heard of it at times, but never seen it myself. What will you do?"

"Dunno yet." He stomped his heel into his boot and looked up, hair sticking up in all directions from her running her fingers through it and even yanking it when she wasn't happy with how he was loving her.

He straightened and jammed his hat on. She shook her head at him.

"What?" He gave her a quizzical smile.

"You climb out of bed and look ready to model for a cowboy magazine."

"Well so do you."

She looked down at herself. Her clothes were wrinkled and she felt a huge tangle on the back of her head. "I need a minute."

"Take two, baby doll. I'll wait."

She went into the bathroom and cleaned herself up. Then she glanced into the mirror. She tipped her head back to look closer at the red marks put there by Foster's beard scruff. It had felt amazing at the time, and now was a pink reminder of all he'd done to her.

She clamped her thighs tighter together. She shouldn't be wanting him again so soon, should she? In a few days on The Boot Knockers Ranch, she'd become a sex addict. When she got home, she'd have to buy herself a crate of toys just to hold her off.

After brushing her teeth and smearing sunscreen over her face, she felt more herself. She walked into the front of the cabin to find Foster holding an energy drink and something wrapped in wax paper that smelled delicious.

"How the heck do you do that?" She accepted them from him.

"You don't think I whipped up this breakfast sandwich, do ya?"

She raised it to her nose, inhaling cheese and egg along with fragrant bacon. "What about yours?"

"Wolfed it down already." He backhanded his lips, which weren't even greasy. "After last night, I needed to refuel." He waggled his brows at her and she laughed.

They set off across the ranch on foot, and she nibbled at the sandwich. After the first bite, she hogged hers down too. When she wadded the paper and stuffed it into her pocket, he sent her a sideways glance. "Good, huh?"

"Delicious. Thank you."

"I like taking care of my lover after I've fucked all the energy from her. Drink up. You'll need it."

She tried to ignore his words. They weren't at all sweet, yet they dug deep into her psyche and she couldn't deny the warmth rising in her. Maybe her sister was right—she was a hopeless romantic. No matter how much armor she heaped on herself, a few words could worm through the cracks and touch her.

They reached a big, old shed with peeling paint, and he rolled back a door. She expected to see broken-down farm equipment, but several new ATVs sat there.

"Wow."

"Tools of the trade in these parts. Don't always have time to saddle up. Can you hold on tight?"

"Yes, but not around your waist."

"Suit yourself." He walked to one and swung his leg over it. She eased on behind him, trying not to wrap her legs around his powerful haunches. He handed her a helmet, and he put one on too.

She gripped the sides of the seat.

"Got a good, strong hold?" He glanced over his shoulder at her.

"Yep."

"Good." He shot out the door. She rocked back and almost tumbled off. She grappled for his middle, wrapping her arms around him so tight that she felt him wheeze out a laugh.

Jerk. He'd done that on purpose. As soon as she looked around at the landscape, though, she forgot to be mad at him. The scene was breathtaking. Rich blues of the mountains in the distance, the sky a pale azure, struck with gold where the sun had risen. And green-gold fields being flattened under the tires of the ATV.

Her family ranch was beautiful but nothing like this. She could easily drop a house right here in this very spot and happily walk outside each day to drink in the view.

As they cut across the field, she spotted the elk. Not a few as she'd guessed, but a massive herd that would easily obliterate the grazing land if they stuck around a day or two. Which would mean real trouble for The Boot Knockers' cattle. Their prime food source would be wiped out until it grew back. But it was also unlikely the elk would head down the mountainside again in this warmer weather.

Foster slowed enough that she could be heard over the engine.

"This is crazy," she said.

"That's an understatement, baby doll."

Several mounted riders and another ATV stood on the edge of where the elk herd grazed. When they approached slowly, she saw she was the only woman in the group. They all tipped their hats to her and offered smiles that weren't remotely flirty — they all seemed stressed by this problem.

Foster didn't coddle her by helping her off the ATV or by holding her hand. He walked up to the guys and started puzzling out the issue, weighing their options.

"Can drive them off," one guy said. He rubbed at the back of his neck, and she saw several hickeys there.

"Unlikely that'll work, at least not for long. They found gold up here and they won't leave until they've eaten their fill," Foster said.

She drifted next to him and stared at the elk.

"Unfortunate it's such a big herd. We could put up with it otherwise." She'd been introduced to this cowboy as Shayne down in the dining hall.

A couple of the others looked to Foster. He seemed to be a natural leader among them, and something oddly like pride rose in Chevy's chest. A stronger wind kicked up, and they all made a grab for their hats to keep them in place, including her. The calls of the elk reached them.

"Lil has to be going off her rocker about this," Foster said.

Shayne shook his head.

"What? You didn't tell her?"

"Hell no, would you? She's crazy enough about what's going on with her ranch and being stuck in the office. We need her down there. That's why we sent for you. Figured you'd know what to do."

"This ranch has been in her family for decades. I'm sure the elk have come before. She'll know what to do."

Chevy bit her lower lip. She had an idea but was unsure her voice would be welcome.

Foster glanced down at her. "What is it?"

"Well elk don't tolerate sheep. If you have any sheep or a neighbor could drive his up here..."

Everyone stared at her. She avoided their gazes and met Foster's. His eyes were burning again, like two torches.

"Brilliant, baby doll." He cupped her cheeks and crushed his lips over hers. She rocked back, stunned at how genuine that action had been.

"Want me to pay a visit to old Mack on the neighboring ranch?" Shayne asked.

"Yup. Take our ATV—it's quicker. We'll get some sheep up here as a natural barrier and hopefully the elk will head elsewhere." Foster reached for Chevy's fingers and squeezed them hard before letting go. "Wyoming, Bastian, take the horses and go with Shayne. The rest of us will stick around here and rig up some sort of enclosure so we don't lose any of Mack's sheep."

"You think he'll lend them?" Chevy asked.

He was filled with excitement. "Yes. This is prime grazing and he'll get back some fat sheep. He's old but not senile."

The ATV fired up and the two men on horseback took off for the neighboring ranch. The rest of them stood clustered talking, but Foster stuck by her.

"That really was a brilliant idea, Chevy."

She felt warmth climb her cheeks but she was pleased with herself. "Thanks."

"You ever consider owning your own spread the way Lil does?"

She chewed her lip again. Did she confess it had always been her dream to own her own ranch and grab a male-dominated industry by the balls?

"Thought of it once or twice," she said quietly.

"Is it out of the range of possibility?" Silhouetted against the sky, he was almost as breathtaking as the landscape. Maybe more so, in this moment.

She lifted a shoulder and let it fall. "I don't have the capital."

"That's just paperwork at the bank."

"Maybe."

He wrapped his fingers around her upper arm and turned her to look at him. "You know you can do it, right?"

"Yes." But her voice didn't reflect that sentiment.

He held her by both arms, hovering over her. His expression was all seriousness. "You're tough enough to ranch. Smart as a whip too. I've never seen anyone so capable next to Lil. And you know one of the biggest ranchers in history was a woman, don't you?"

She shook her head.

"In the 1800s a woman named Margaret Heffernan Borland came West and she owned more than 10,000 cattle in Texas."

She snorted a laugh. "That's a lot more than I'd want to handle."

"Right, but I'm just saying. If you wanted to, you could."

She dragged in a deep breath, scented like the outdoors and Foster. He stood so close, and if she went on tiptoe she could kiss the hell out of him for believing in her this way. She didn't, though.

"Thank you for pushing me toward my dream."

His smile was soft, his eyes softer. He drew her closer and instead of kissing her, pressed his lips between her brows. A tender brushing of his mouth that left her more shaken than if he'd shoved his tongue down her throat.

He got called away to speak with the other Boot Knockers, which was good. She needed a moment to collect herself and pick her heart up off the ground. But as she listened to him discuss the ranch operations, she only liked him more.

An hour or so later, an older gentleman came up the hill to negotiate. Foster stepped up to do the talking, and Chevy listened, enraptured by how capable he was. He negotiated like a lawyer. And why not? Hell, he'd probably been to law school.

When everything was settled and hands shaken, Foster turned to her. "I'm going on to drive the sheep up here. Can you take one of the horses and go back? I'll meet you there."

She could drive as well as anyone else, but she didn't want to stick her foot in the door where she wasn't welcome. She nodded.

He gripped her elbow before she could turn away. "Wait for me. Don't put up any walls while I'm gone." He yanked her in and kissed her — hard. She sucked in a gasp, and he navigated her mouth with his tongue.

When he pulled away, she was left dazed. Her legs shook as she made her way to one of the horses. She took a minute to allow the mount to sniff her before she took her seat in the saddle.

Don't put up any walls.

She didn't know if she liked him probing so deep in her mind. That he even knew her well enough to say she did throw up barriers stunned her.

All her resistance tactics obviously weren't working. As she trotted back to the ranch, over the beautiful land, she thought up a plan. She'd turn the tables on the Candlelight Cowboy and see if she could romance him. It would give her the reins.

He saw her as in control enough to run a ranch of her own. It was time to show him she could be in charge of her entire life, especially the relationship part.

Chapter Seven

When Foster walked through the door of the cabin, music reached him. Some old country ballads that stirred a nostalgia in him. With a smile, he closed the door and looked around the space.

Chevy had found what looked like every candle in the place and they stood on every surface, throwing their light and giving off a sweet fragrance.

Not as sweet as her, though. He caught the notes of her body wash and his cock started to harden. Sweet Jesus, this woman was going to kill him. He was always a horny motherfucker, but this was ridiculous. He couldn't even think about her without growing hard.

"Chevy?"

"In here."

He walked through the rooms. She wasn't lying on the bed wearing some frilly negligee as he expected. Whatever she had planned was going to be a first for him. The ladies he'd wooed didn't return the favor, and that was fine by him. He couldn't say he wasn't excited to be on the receiving end, though.

He stepped through the bathroom door. The space was aglow with warm candlelight. And she'd drawn a bath. Steam rose off the water, which was a bright blue color.

He laughed and plucked off his hat. "How'd you know blue's my favorite color?"

"You wear a lot of blue shirts." She sat on the edge of the tub wearing a silky robe. Definitely dressed for seduction.

"I like the music."

"Do you?" When he'd last seen her, she'd been fresh-faced without a hint of makeup. Now she was dolled up, her lashes long and curled, her lips the color of a rosebud.

He took her hand and raised her to her feet. "I do."

The strains of an old George Jones song filled the cabin. Chevy looked sensual and gorgeous, and he couldn't wait to sink into her sweet body.

He towed her into his arms, and she curled against him, arms around his neck. He started to sway, looking down into her eyes. The slip of her silky robe against her bare skin underneath made him bite back a moan.

He danced her out of the bathroom and through the bedroom, circling like a pro.

"How do you know how to dance? Don't tell me you have a degree in that too."

"No, but I took lessons in college."

She giggled. "Let me guess—there was a woman involved."

He whisked her into a reverse spin and then dipped her. His lips an inch away from her succulent throat, he dragged in a deep breath of her personal scent. Damn, she was amazing. How had she managed to keep a ring off her finger for this long? Any man would be smitten by her.

And he wasn't easily smitten.

The notion sobered him. "A woman was involved in the lessons, but I'm glad I took them."

"You like showing off."

"I like feeling you in my arms."

At that, her eyelids fluttered. She didn't want the sugar-coated words, but he couldn't seem to help himself. They rolled off his tongue, unpracticed. More genuine than they'd ever been.

"Did you get the sheep situated?"

"Yes. Took some doing. Mack's got some wayward beasts."

She hesitated, color flooding her cheeks. "And... did it work?"

He gave a single nod. What she'd suggested had been a genius move. "The elk herd's already moving down the hillside. Thank you. And Lil thanks you too."

"You told her about it? I thought you weren't going to trouble her."

"In the end, I knew when she found out she'd be irate to be left out of the goings-on around here. It's her place, after all. The Boot Knockers just pay her a hefty fee to operate up here."

"Have you ever been to the Texas ranch?"

"Yep. Whoooeee, those guys are a wild bunch. Makes us seem tame."

"Tame? I saw a couple fucking on a picnic table in broad daylight."

He made a noise of dismissal. "That's just normal exhibitionist behavior."

"What do you consider spicier behavior?"

"When there's more than five people involved." Her eyes popped, and he laughed. "Would you ever participate in something like that?"

"I don't know. Probably not. I don't think there are two people out there who would want to be with me. I take it you have done it."

"Sometimes sex is sex. It's fun."

"And the other times?"

As he let his gaze travel over her perfect complexion under the candle's glow, his chest tightened. Last night watching her come apart for him several times... Well, it had been his one and only drive in life. He forgot all his other duties and made Chevy the center of his universe.

On the ATV today, her arms cinching him in half and her solid warmth against his back, he'd given their situation more thought. He hadn't felt this way before, not even with nonclients.

Maybe he was just getting better at his job, more attuned to the client. That had to be it. When he'd told her not to throw up any walls while he was gone, he'd seen his words hit home. She'd blinked as if shocked that he'd read her so easily, seen through her.

And her decision to romance him, to reverse the roles here tonight... He saw through that too. She wanted to be in control, and he'd let her.

For now.

He lightly pinched the point of her delicate chin and looked into her eyes. "Should I get into that tub of hot water before it cools off?"

"Yes. You smell." She pushed against his chest.

He laughed and let her go. She drifted to the bathroom door to watch him strip and climb into the water. It was slightly cooler, so he turned on the taps again, flooding it with hot.

"Come sit on the ledge and talk to me."

He didn't want her to go. He wanted to share his day, what had happened with Mack and the sheep. How he and Wyoming had chased after a few who'd broken away from the herd and he'd had to use his tie-down roping skills.

Damn, how had he ended up sitting in the hot water talking about himself while Chevy listened? This was getting personal. He'd never spoken of his love of the ranch with any other women.

She sank to the ledge and put a bottle of body wash into his hand. He laughed. "That bad, huh?"

"You smell like horse and manure."

He told her about the escapade he and Wyoming had shared with the sheep, watching her smile and laugh at him. After he'd soaped up, he scooted down in the big tub to dunk his head. When he came up, water streaming off his face, Chevy was too beautiful, too heart-stopping, not to act.

He hooked her around the middle and reeled her into the water.

* * * * *

She hit his lap with a splash, hot water drenching her robe so it clung obscenely to her breasts, the outlines visible, as were her hard nipples.

"Uh! What'd you do that for?"

"Because I wanted you right here." He pulled her down onto his erection, and she stilled at the sensation of his steel digging into her backside. It was difficult enough looking at it when he'd taken off his clothes, but now her self-control was out the window.

She ground against him, and he groaned. He placed his lips close to her ear. "You think you can tease a man like me, Chevy?"

"I can rule you if I want."

130

He breathed a laugh that tickled her earlobe. "You already do." He took her hand and moved it between their bodies so she felt just how much she ruled him.

She tipped her head back to look at him, and her heart beat faster. For a second, she embraced the warm, tickling feeling he gave her all over. Then she realized what she was doing.

Crap. Her plan had backfired on her. She'd hoped to control all that happened tonight, but here she sat, at his mercy in a tub of water, on his lap.

He rocked his hips, drilling his cock between her thighs. One slip and he'd join with her. Her pussy throbbed for it. If they were in a committed relationship, she'd shimmy down over his length without—

What was she thinking? She'd lost her mind, for sure. This was Foster. A man who fucked women for a living. She was nothing to him.

"Hey." He cupped her jaw, the rough pads of his fingers toying with the sensitive spot behind her ear. "What's that look for?"

She glanced away. "Nothing."

He palmed her cheek and her breast at the same time. Liquid warmth pooled low in her belly. He captured her gaze as he strummed her nipple lightly with his thumb. Back and forth over the hard peak until she felt a quivering begin deep inside.

She let her head fall back, and he kissed her throat. Licking the water drops off and turning his lips into hers with a ferocity that stunned her. It almost felt like… passion.

Shaking off the thought, she allowed her body to take over. Each sensation was heightened sitting in the water this way, and his touch on her nipple was no longer enough.

She pressed his hand against her harder. "Pinch it."

He groaned and rolled her tight bud between his thumb and forefinger until she thought she'd lose her mind. Then he ducked his head and bit into it like a ripe cherry. She cried out, wiggling closer to his warmth. His cock slid over her slippery folds. It would only take one slip. One movement to the side, and he'd be with her. Fucking her.

She held completely still as he nipped at her breast and then turned to the other. She watched his eyes close and wondered what a man like Foster thought or felt while doing this to a woman. He seemed really into it, and for now she wouldn't let herself think of him being with scores of other women. And she sure as hell wasn't thinking of him belonging to *her*.

They were in this moment together, and she'd take everything she could from it. The pressure between her thighs became unbearable. Her pussy throbbed steadily, and she wanted — needed — more.

She twisted in his arms to straddle him. His eyes widened as the head of his cock rested at her opening.

"Fuck, I want you," he rasped.

Tingles traveled over her spine and shoulders. "Not yet," she whispered against his lips and started using her hands to cup water and pour it over his soapy flesh.

When he was rinsed, it was clear he wasn't waiting longer. He stood up, water pouring off his chiseled form, and lifted her. She dangled there, legs hooked over his strong forearm, her soaking wet robe clinging to her skin.

"Fucking hell, you're beautiful." He claimed her lips in a kiss so searing she didn't recall him leaving the tub or carrying her to the bed. Or of him stripping away her wet robe.

She lay on the bed staring up at him, wondering how the hell this man had bewitched her more than all the others put together. Then he donned a condom and slid home, and she stopped caring.

* * * * *

"Come for me. Come on my cock again." He grunted his urges into her ear with each mind-blowing stroke. Chevy's legs were slung over his shoulders, her pussy at the perfect angle, clenched around him like a fucking fist.

He was addicted to watching her features contort with erotic pleasure. He couldn't get enough of her rasping cries or the way she looked up at him when she came down from a high. He felt more powerful from every orgasm she gave him.

She tightened, started to shake. He knew she was on the cusp of orgasm. He turned his head and sucked the flesh of her calf into his mouth. Churning his hips until he felt his cock buried so deep that he had to bite back his own release.

A dew of perspiration coated her throat as she threw her head back and screamed her release. He pounded into her, drawing moan after moan from her sweet lips. When she lay gasping, he unhooked her ankles from his shoulders and leaned down to kiss her. She melted in his embrace—tucked so close he had no idea where he ended anymore—and kissed him back.

After another heartbeat or two, he pulled out and rolled her onto her stomach. She lay there flat, as if unable to move. He bit back a chuckle and grasped her hips. Pulling her ass up was a mistake, because he almost shot his load then and there.

He fisted his cock hard to hold back, and only when he was in control again did he run his hands over her backside.

"Such a perfect ass. I want to fuck it so bad. Or watch Wyoming take you here while I fuck your tight pussy."

"Oh God. Foster…" Her breaths came faster.

He plastered his body to her spine. "Does that turn you on?" he asked in her ear. She shivered. "I can tell it does. Will you let me share you with him before the week's out? I want to show you the pleasure two men can give you." He wanted to hoard her moans and her dazed looks in his memory and pull them out later when he was feeling lonely.

He pushed out a breath. He rarely admitted to loneliness. He had tons of friends and lovers. With all the work he did around here, he didn't have time to think about more. But Chevy had yanked that cord inside him, and now the water bucket had fallen on his head to drench him with the knowledge that yes, he was lonely. He craved an intimate connection, and damn if she wasn't giving it to him.

"Will you let me spread your pussy with my cock while he sinks into your ass? I want you to be so full, so fucking turned on for us, that you can't stop coming."

"Foster… Oh God, I want that."

He thumbed her anus and she pushed up against his touch. He slipped his hand under her to flick her clit too. It stiffened and he ground it against her body. He teased her in both spots until she was on the verge of climax again.

Before she reached it, he moved his hands back to her hips, angled her upward and sank into her body in one quick glide.

She threw her head back and wiggled down on his cock, taking all of him. Right to the balls.

Warm, wet heat enveloped him, tearing away the last thread of his control. He watched himself slide in and out and alternated with looking at her beautiful face. Lips parted on a gasp, her eyes squeezed shut, her cheeks flushed as he drove her to a climax that rattled the headboard off the wall.

It fucking rattled him too.

He pushed deep and exploded with a roar.

* * * * *

When Chevy woke, she moaned. She was stiff and pleasantly sore from everything Foster had done to her last night. At one point, their position had seemed more like gymnastics than bed play. But she'd never felt so satisfied.

She heard the shower switch off and a couple minutes later, he emerged from the bathroom in a cloud of steam. She wished he wasn't so damn attractive. She'd never be able to accept someone vanilla like her sister's fiancé now.

Speaking of vanilla, Foster hadn't really meant what he'd said about sharing her with Wyoming, had he? Her nipples were hard just thinking about it.

Foster noticed too. He gave her one of his crooked grins and scuffed his knuckles over his unshaven cheek. "I'm heading up to check on the sheep. Wanna come?"

Yes, she did. She liked being with him, and that was why she had to decline. She shook her head, and a small frown appeared between his brows.

He came to the bed and leaned over to kiss her lightly. "Okay. Stay here and sleep. I'll be back for you in an hour or so."

She wanted to respond by saying she looked forward to it. But she had to find the strength to build that wall again. Sometime in the night, he'd torn it down. The bricks were in a heap, scattered around her. How had it happened? She was actually daydreaming of this being their cabin and him coming home to her.

She sat up and ran her fingers through her hair. *That's it. No more bubble baths or sweet words about how capable I am to run a ranch of my own.*

"I'll see you later," she said in a breezy, noncommittal way.

He stared at her as if trying to puzzle out what he'd done to cause this change in her. It wasn't his fault, though. He was Foster—just being himself. It wasn't his problem that she was a lunatic romantic, foisting herself on every man who looked at her that way.

Except no man had ever looked at her the way Foster was.

She hopped out of bed and practically chased him out the door. When it was firmly closed and his bulging back muscles safely out of sight, she leaned against the wall and took a deep breath.

Why did ignoring him suddenly seem harder than anything she'd ever done in her life?

* * * * *

Foster swung by the lodge to grab a cold drink before heading out to work on the ranch. On the way past the cabins, he didn't run into a single Boot Knocker or lady. Later in the week, couples tended to stick to themselves. Then by the end of the week, things got hot and dirty.

As he rode out, the morning breeze was cool, and he welcomed it. Since last night, he felt like he was riding a horse wearing three shoes. The only reason he had for feeling this way was Chevy.

He was back to trying to figure her out. Last night had been amazing, even for him. He always threw himself into loving a woman and showing her how important she was, but—

"You look lost in thought." Shayne's voice brought his head around. His buddy was coming out of the kitchen carrying a big picnic basket.

Foster raised his chin toward the basket. "You headin' out for the day?"

"Yep, ATV ride. Michaela doesn't trust horses."

"Sounds good. Nice day for it."

Shayne narrowed his eyes at Foster. "What's up with you?"

"What do you mean?" His hand was wet with condensation from the water bottle he held and he wiped it on his jeans.

"You never talk about mundane shit like weather unless it's got to do with the ranch work. What's eating at you?"

Foster compressed his lips. Did he share his thoughts with Shayne? He was as close-lipped as a nun in church. But Foster hadn't totally figured it out for himself yet, so how could he tell somebody else?

"Is it your lady? She seems mighty headstrong."

"Yeah, and that's a good thing. She's keeping me on my toes. Nothing easy about her."

"That's the trouble?" Shayne set the basket on a nearby table.

Foster shook his head. "I like the challenge. No fun to do the same thing over and over again. I just don't know if I'm breaking through to her or not."

Shayne stared at him, waiting. His buddy knew when to shut his mouth and listen, and Foster was grateful for it.

"I want her to know how important and beautiful she is. How much she has to offer the world and somebody special if she chooses. I try hard and mean everything I say and do with every woman who comes here. But somehow this feels different. Like if I don't make Chevy understand then I can't go on."

Shayne just stared at him.

"What? Oh fuck, you think I'm crazy."

He shook his head. "No. I think you're falling for her."

Foster rocked back on his boots as if Shayne had punched him. The air left his lungs, and he dropped his head, trying to recover.

"The signs are all there, man. Think about it."

Foster didn't know what to say. He hadn't fallen for a woman in a very long time—so long that he might not remember what it felt like.

It feels like this.

But they'd only met a few days ago, and most of those had been spent mulling over the wrong turns he was making with her.

He couldn't be falling for Chevy.

He shook himself and straightened. "Gotta check on the sheep."

"Want me to join you before I go picnic?"

"Nah, you enjoy yourself. I got it." He needed the time alone too. Even being around Chevy right now would confuse him more.

He jolted again. Chevy had practically kicked him out of the cabin and slammed the door behind him. Could she need the time alone to figure out her emotions too?

A vision of her looking up at him with a blissed-out expression on her face filled his mind. As he'd sunk into her again and again, he'd captured her gaze and held it prisoner. She hadn't looked away once, even when her thready cry sounded at the last. That connection wasn't something that occurred often.

Hell, ever.

If he was falling, so was she. He threw a wave at Shayne and headed out of the lodge. Each step he took to the barn, and every motion he made to ready his mount was automatic, because his brain was back in Cabin 3.

He'd never had a woman give him a blue bubble bath. Or fuck, blue balls the way she had. And riding and walking the fence line became something special. He even enjoyed her company when she friend-zoned him.

He had a few more days with her. Sunday morning she'd return to her life. His job was to make her confident and ready for anything that came at her from a relationship standpoint, but damn if he wanted her to have one.

Oh yeah, jealousy was a sure sign he was in deeper than he thought. His boots were mired in quicksand and he was sinking quick. Did he have a chance to pull out? He could put on the brakes and end the week without the same intimacy they'd achieved, but the notion made him ache.

All he could do was go on, grab life by the balls and experience all the thrills with her. He'd make every minute of her stay filled with more excitement and hotter sex. Because after Sunday he'd be left wanting, and he guessed it would be for a very long time. She wasn't a woman you got over easy.

* * * * *

As they rounded the corner of the shed, Chevy's jaw dropped. Ten ATVs sat there on the edge of a muddy, rutted field. She looked to Foster. "When you told me to wear something I could get dirty, I thought you were just trying to seduce me."

"Who says I'm not?" He dropped her that panties-melting crooked smile. "C'mon. I see a four-wheeler with our names on it." He took off toward the group clustered around the vehicles and she had no choice but to follow.

She really hadn't dressed for riding through the muck. Why hadn't she listened to Foster?

Because I was being stubborn.

Now she was going to ruin her favorite jeans.

When he looked around and saw she hadn't moved from her original spot, he came back to her, that crease between his brows. "All right?" he asked.

"I'm not sure I want to do this. I wore my favorite jeans and I don't want to ruin them."

"So take 'em off."

She opened her mouth to protest and then saw how scantily clad some of the other ladies were. One was dressed only in a bra and underwear. One a tank top and tiny shorts.

Did she have the confidence to strip down in front of all these people? Better yet, did she have the stamina to get on an ATV behind the

145

man she was burning for already with only a thin barrier of satin to shield her? Satin that would get splashed with mud and the water in the deep ruts.

"I don't know." Her voice sounded wobbly and she hated herself for it. She'd come to The Boot Knockers Ranch for more than to overcome her relationship problems—she wanted some fun experiences, to get out of her comfort zone.

This was her chance.

Under his steady, warm gaze, she reached for the button of her jeans. She popped it open, and he cracked a smile in the way only a country boy could.

Next she unzipped. She glanced around. Nobody was paying any attention to her, and it wasn't a lot different from wearing a bikini to the beach. Not that she did that often in Montana.

Foster waited to see what she'd do. She bent to remove her boots and socks. Then she swallowed hard and shoved her jeans down.

Several whoops sounded, and her face heated to the temperature of a roasted chicken, but she managed to straighten and allow Foster to take her hand.

"Sure you wanna ruin the top?"

"Jerk." She bit back a giggle that was part nervous horror at her own actions. Who knew she was such a prude, too? Maybe coming to the ranch would teach her more about herself than she'd originally thought.

"I'm ready," she said.

"Hold on." With his hot stare fixing her to the earth, he reached for his own waistband. His belt clinked as he flicked it open. She couldn't help but react to him undressing. Mmmm, those strong hands with the veins on the backs working over his fly.

When he shoved off his boots, socks and jeans, leaving him only in a pair of black briefs, more catcalls sounded, from men and women alike.

"Now I'm ready." He grabbed Chevy's hand and yanked her to the edge of the field. There was a little turf left here that hadn't been torn up by tires, but water and mud still squished up between her bare toes.

Couples started climbing onto the ATVs and Foster strode up to one, hauling her behind him. A sexy man wearing only a pair of navy boxer briefs was about to throw his leg over the seat.

"Not so fast, Wyoming." Foster caught him by the balls—literally. He cupped his privates and Wyoming twisted with one leg in the air, hovering over the seat. "This is mine."

"Don't see your name on it, Fos. Appreciate it if you'd let go of my nuts."

More laughter from around them as the other Boot Knockers watched.

"You know I always get the one with the blue stripe."

"Wasn't written into the mud. I got here first." He gyrated his hips to try to dislodge Foster's hand.

Chevy looked between his legs and saw that Foster wasn't really gripping him by the nuts as much as fondling them. Dark heat slithered between her thighs. This was the man Foster had mentioned sharing her with.

She raked her gaze over Wyoming's body—big, bulging in all the right places and he sported a square jaw that invited a girl to touch it.

Was this some kind of foreplay? She couldn't help but think it was. Her nipples bunched under her T-shirt.

Foster ran his thumb over the bulge between Wyoming's legs.

"A little more of that and you might convince me to find another ATV."

"That's the plan." Foster squeezed Chevy's fingers, which he still held in his other hand. Linking the three of them. Oh God, if she went through with this sharing stuff, she'd never be the same.

A beautiful woman with long blonde hair and wearing a brown cowgirl hat strode in front of the line of ATVs. "Get ready, ladies and Boot Knockers!"

This must be Lil. Chevy pulled her stare away from her lover's hands on another man and directed her attention toward the woman who owned the ranch and was acting as office manager right now.

Lil shot Wyoming and Foster a look, and Wyoming dropped to the seat, trapping Foster's hand. Everyone who saw laughed, and Foster made a show of yanking his hand free. He led Chevy to the only free four-wheeler and climbed on. She got behind him, donned a helmet and this time was smart enough to wrap her arms tightly around his middle. She wasn't taking any chances at being thrown off in the mud while other ATVs zoomed by.

Lil raised a hand with a red kerchief dangling from it. She looked down the line of people revving to go and then dropped her arm. They shot off, and Chevy squealed.

She bit down on her lower lip, not wanting to sound like such a girly wimp, but she heard other ladies scream too. Foster crisscrossed the field, and mud splattered up over Chevy's bare calves.

He cut hard to the right, past another couple, and one thick dollop of mud sprayed onto his torso inches from Chevy's fingers. That must have been the cue to take off after them, because Foster turned the ATV on a dime and hit the gas.

Chevy couldn't help but laugh at what they were doing. She hadn't had so much fun in years, and doing it with Foster felt great. He tapped into a more playful side of her. Not only was she a hopeless romantic and a prude, but she was uptight. She was learning all kinds of things about herself on this vacation.

No question about it—she would return home a different person. She'd experienced too much to be the same old Chevy. She wondered how she'd ever be able to go back to her boring routine with no end in sight.

They whipped past a couple, hurling mud over both, leaving the woman with brown streaks in her honey-blonde hair and the Boot Knocker with a mouthful of mud. He leaned over and spat, and Chevy felt Foster's ribs quake with his laughter.

Now it seemed they had several couples gunning for them. Foster had to punch it to get away, but after several passes through the field, Chevy was soaking wet, laughing like a loon and caked in mud.

There was a loud horn honk that brought everyone around. Foster rolled into line again next to the other ATVs. Chevy released her tight hold on his waist and found that where her arms had been, his skin was clean and smooth and tanned, while everything else was dirty.

"Cleanest couple wins! Line up, everybody," Lil called.

Foster cut the engine. When Chevy planted her foot on the ground, she expected it to stay there, but she sank up to her ankle and fell over.

She floundered for a second before strong arms plucked her out and set her on her feet.

"All right, baby doll?" He chuckled.

151

"We're definitely not the cleanest now."

"Nope, you took care of that." He grinned, his teeth the whitest, cleanest part of his face.

Lil walked down the line, judging how dirty they were. Two people were pulled out of the line. A woman with short curly hair and a sweet face stood proudly next to her Boot Knocker, who was tall and as toned as an athlete. They grasped hands and held them up in the air. Cheers sounded.

Then Lil shoved them and they fell into the mud. Several cowboys jumped on top of them, squashing them in good. Chevy laughed until her sides hurt.

Wyoming went to give them a hand up and ended up getting yanked in too.

"Go help them," Chevy encouraged Foster.

He leveled his dark, amused stare on her, leaving her with a sizzling feeling in her lower parts. "You realize we'll need another bath and you're getting in with me."

"We'll clog the drain like this." She looked down at herself. In the end, she didn't have to worry about modesty because her lower half was so filthy nobody could see her panties. Nor did they care.

She wasn't about to get into the tub with Foster again, though. Last time had ended in disaster—for her heart. Her *stupid* heart. So easily sucked in, so fragile.

"I can turn the garden hose on you. Or we can jump into the stock tank."

"And contaminate all that drinking water for the animals? No way."

The unfortunate couple who'd won was dragged from the mud and put onto a four-wheeler to do more turns through the field as their victory parade. Some couples broke off, walking back to the cabins to get cleaned up… and more.

Chevy noticed Wyoming was standing not far off, barely listening to another Boot Knocker because he was staring at her.

A shiver ran through her. Had Foster mentioned sharing her? He must have. Or maybe it was an unspoken deal between the friends.

Would she let it happen? Could she stop it? The idea turned her on—no, it lit her up like a firework on the Fourth of July. A few touches and kisses and she'd shoot off like a roman candle.

Foster followed her path of sight and gave her a knowing smile. "Let's head back to the cabin and get cleaned up."

Chapter Eight

Foster made a move to drop his clean clothes and boots in the yard in front of the cabin and then stopped.

"What are you doing?"

"Don't want to give housekeeping more work. Hold it. Can you walk in bare feet?"

She blinked, those long lashes of hers distracting the hell out of him. "Depends on where we're going."

Chevy gave a shiver.

"Cold?" he asked.

She bit down on her lower lip to stop a rueful smile. "Grossed out. This mud feels disgusting, you know… down there." She looked to his crotch.

"You're right, baby doll. It's a short walk. C'mon."

He grabbed her by the hand. Entwining his fingers with hers was as natural as breathing. He led her out of the yard and in the opposite direction of the lodge.

"Where are we going?" Her hair curled at her temples from perspiration, and the dew on her throat made him think dirtier thoughts.

"You'll see. You look damn cute when you're covered in mud."

Pink roses bloomed on her cheeks. "You say that to all the girls." She threw him a mischievous look.

He tossed his head back and laughed. "I've never seen someone who can wear a smudge of mud on her nose so well."

Horror crossed her face. She stopped walking, jerked her hand from his and cupped her nose. "What? You're kidding." She started to scrub at it. He watched her for a moment and then very deliberately, holding her gaze, licked the pad of his thumb.

She backed up a step.

"Let me get that."

"Don't you dare."

He stepped up to her and caught her wrists. He gently tugged her hand away from her face and leaned in. He softly kissed the tip of her nose.

Breath rushed from her. "I thought you said it's dirty."

"I was teasin'. It's perfectly clean. Now you do have a smear of mud here." He brushed his lips just under the outline of her cheekbone. A shiver tore through her, and this time he didn't ask if she was cold. He knew otherwise.

Before she could say more, he meshed their hands again and led her away. It was just a short walk to their destination, and he was sure she didn't know where they were going. She hadn't explored the ranch that thoroughly, and he still had a trick or two up his sleeve.

He hoped nobody else had chosen this spot—he wanted to be alone with Chevy. Her modesty would keep her from enjoying sex in public. And he wasn't so sure he wanted another Boot Knocker looking at her anyway.

Besides Wyoming. He'd seen his friend eyeing Chevy back at the field. Actually, his balls had tightened at the idea of that man going down between her thighs and licking her pussy on Foster's command.

He didn't need to share her to find a thrill, though. Hell, just looking at her did that. He wanted to show her how two men could worship her until she lay limp.

As soon as the pond came into view, Chevy let out a sigh. "Oh my God, it's beautiful."

He looked at the view through her eyes. The blue of the sky sat like a thick band atop a rolling expanse of green land. In the center was a pool of water, the edges uneven with a bit of growth around the edge. A few birds flitted around it, swooping toward the water and then soaring again.

She glanced at the ground. "I don't see any cattle tracks."

"They can't get this far. The fences keep them back. It's clean water. Good for swimmin'." He searched her gaze, delving deeper into her eyes than he had yet. Damn, her eyes were slaying him.

He couldn't deny the sweet warmth flooding his chest. A week ago he hadn't known more than her name. Now it rang in his head like a gong. She was tossing lasso after lasso at him, making him dodge and scamper to avoid falling back on tricks that didn't work on her.

She swayed forward, and he wrapped her against his chest. He ran his lips over her hair, warm from the sun, and just drank in the moment. A gorgeous view and an amazing woman in his arms.

He never could have gotten such satisfaction using his multiple degrees. His family and friends had questioned his motives in dropping everything to come to The Boot Knockers Ranch. But it was the best decision of his life. The world didn't always make sense until you tried it out.

Right now, Chevy made sense. Right here, molded to him.

She made a quiet sound and he drew back to look at her. Her brow was furrowed, and he figured she was overthinking something. Before she could let the thought run wild in her pretty little head, he swept her off her feet and took off running toward the water.

"Don't throw me in!" She giggled wildly.

He set her on her feet and walked right into the water.

* * * * *

Watching a big cowboy cut through the water in a smooth sidestroke was sexy as hell. But seeing him emerge, soaked boxers hanging low enough on his hips that the ring of muscle between hips and abs was visible, was damn breathtaking.

Chevy stared at Foster. The sun beamed down on his tanned, glistening skin. Defining each dip and swell of his chest and arms. His abs…whoooeee. When a woman thought of the perfect physique, she pictured abs like Foster's.

She swallowed hard, trying to still her quivering insides. This wasn't a bath by candlelight and Foster wasn't giving her the smoldering look. His lips were curled up in mischief, and she knew he was about to dunk her.

She swam a few feet away, but he still managed to nab her by the ankle. She squealed and he reeled her in like a fish on a line. His cool fingers traveled up her ankle to her knee. Her nipples and pussy throbbed.

"Let go," she cried without any real dedication to getting away.

"No. Stop. Help," he said dryly. Then he slid his fingers right up between her legs. She floundered, unable to float from the sudden tension running through her body. Those fingertips were the point of all pleasure, and she wanted it bad.

He scooped an arm under her shoulders and guided her onto her back. "You're mighty muddy, baby doll. How 'bout I help you get some of it off?" His eyes darkened, and a few drops of water trickled down his face.

She stared at him, heart pumping. Dammit, she liked everything about him.

He eased his fingers under her panties and found her clit. She gasped and he pulled her closer, anchoring her to him.

"I've never been—" her breath hitched as he found the bundle of nerves that sent erotic pleasure flowing over her, "fingered while floating before."

"Never tried it either, but it seems to be working fine." He didn't move his hot gaze from hers as he circled her swollen bud. The cool water against her aching nerve endings electrified her.

Then he splayed his fingers and sank one into her pussy while trapping her clit beneath the other. She shook in his hold, creating ripples in the water.

"You're so fucking hot," he bit off as he plunged his finger in and out of her. She'd been on the verge of orgasm since setting foot on the ranch, and it wouldn't take long to get

161

her there. She didn't bother withholding her cries either. Out here, no one would hear her. And it seemed fitting to share her bliss with this beautiful world and more beautiful man.

He added a second thick, callused finger to her pussy and ground her clit into her body. She wanted him to kiss her badly, but moving was out of the question. She. Was. So. Close.

His gaze seemed to blur with passion as he stared into her eyes. Her heart thudded and her pussy clamped down on his fingers.

"That's it. Fuck. So fucking beautiful. Come for me, baby doll." His command shot through her, and need spiked. She trembled as he stroked her clit one last time... and then exploded.

Waves of pleasure stole her mind for long minutes, but she focused on the man holding her, giving her what she wanted—needed. He slowed his touch, drawing light circles around her still-throbbing bud.

"I think you're muddy here too." He twisted his wrist, removing his finger from her clit. Keeping his middle finger still deep in her pussy, he began to tease her ass with his thumb.

If someone had told her she could come back to back in seconds, she would have thought they were nuts. But the minute he applied pressure to her forbidden spot, she splintered again.

* * * * *

Fuck, she was so responsive, and his cock was in a stranglehold inside his wet boxers. He needed to get them off fast. And find a condom. Everything inside him screamed to just take her, stake his claim. But he couldn't.

He removed his fingers from her pulsating body and let her float while he attacked his jeans. He always had a strip of condoms in his back pocket, and he pulled them out with a wicked grin.

"How long do you plan to keep me here?" She was all soft, ready for him. If he took her ass, she'd be loose. But not yet. Not here.

When he reached into his boxers and pulled his cock out, she flipped her feet down to the sandy bottom of the pond. She was submerged to her breasts, and her top clung to the firm mounds.

His hands shook as he worked the condom over his rigid cock. He needed inside her — now.

"I've come twice and you're behind, Foster." She reached for her breasts and the sharp points at the centers. As she pinched her nipples, he groaned.

"I plan to remedy that right now." With the condom rolled to the base of his shaft, he came toward her. She'd floated a little bit away but not far enough that he couldn't snag her. He yanked the side of her thong and the string snapped.

She made a hissing noise.

"They were ruined anyway." He flashed a grin as he drew her up into his arms, straddling him. Sweet Jesus, she felt so good.

"Look at me while I sink into you." His voice came out gritty.

His aching head was at her entrance, her heat so enveloping it blinded him. He jerked his hips and let her slide down in his arms. She sucked in a harsh gasp as he filled her. He drove back the roar threatening to break free and found her lips. She angled her head and he swiped his tongue through her mouth, deeper with each pass.

The pressure had been building inside him for too long. Feeling her slippery with mud while seated behind him tormented, but after seeing her come apart for him—

He groaned and broke the kiss so he could look at her beautiful face when she shattered again.

Fuck, the men she'd been with were idiots. It had only taken him a few days to figure her out. She didn't hate romance—she hated the cheesy romantic gestures that weren't genuine. But going at it in a pond like wild animals was just fiiiiine.

She wrapped her arms tighter around his shoulders and looked into his eyes. God, that expression... he was teetering on the verge of orgasm in a heartbeat.

"I'm too close. I can't hold out," he rasped.

"Then don't."

"I want you coming with me."

Her breath warmed his cheek. "Then kiss me."

He turned his lips into hers again with a new urgency. Stoking her fires, driving her to moan and writhe until he could hold back no longer. He let go with a low growl and she tightened around him. As soon as the first spurt left him, she clamped down with a cry.

* * * * *

Chevy stretched out on the bank of the pond, her head resting on Foster's damp chest. They were completely nude and the sun and his skin warmed her. If she let her mind touch on the fact that this was pretty damn romantic, she would get angry with herself. But she felt too good to bother.

He drew lazy circles up her arm to her shoulder and back to her elbow, his breathing was deep and even.

She'd satisfied him too.

She didn't bother to curb the smile at the corners of her mouth. Screw it—this was a vacation, and she wasn't going to worry about her past or future right now. She had no idea if she'd smartened up about romance or fallen more into its clutches. All she knew she was having fun and would never be the same.

"Have you thought about stayin' on another week?" His voice made her jerk, and his question shocked her.

"Do women do that?"

"Not really. I was just thinkin'."

166

A thrill ran through her, and her fingers tingled. She wanted to sit up and look at his face to see if he was teasing her, but she didn't dare. If he was as serious as he sounded, it would hook her heart so fast, she'd have no chance in hell of recovering.

She tried to steady her voice. "I don't have the funds to cover another week."

"But if I could take care of that for you, you would?"

Dear God, what was going on in this beautiful man's mind? She pushed onto her elbow to look down at his face. He turned his gaze on her, locked her in it, gave her goosebumps.

She had no idea how to respond. Did she even want to stay another week with Foster?

Hell yes. She was just getting to know him and she'd soon be leaving. It was worse than a one-night stand because she'd had enough time to get attached. Maybe he was getting attached too, and—

She stomped on her thoughts and counted to thirty before answering.

"I'm needed at home soon. My sister's getting married, and there's a shower I have to throw for her."

167

His Adam's apple bulged against his throat as he swallowed. He didn't speak.

She ran her gaze over his face, the features so precise and beautiful, they looked as if they'd been put there by hammer and chisel.

"Are you happy here on the ranch, Foster?"

A cloud passed over the sun, darkening his face. At least she thought it was the cloud that caused the shadows.

"I love this ranch."

"Before this, were you using one of your many degrees?"

He shook his head. "I worked for a while for a big corporation in the financial department, but I cracked one day and just walked out. Never looked back."

"Where did you go?"

"Traveled for a while until I crossed paths with a rancher in Colorado. He took me on and I started learning the ropes."

"You didn't grow up ranching?"

The corner of his lips begged for her to kiss him when he smiled, but she resisted. "Does that surprise you?"

"Definitely. You know your way around cattle like you were born in boots."

He chuckled, low, spreading another layer of gooseflesh over her skin that had just smoothed out. "Maybe I was, and all the searching I did for a career was for nothing."

"Makes sense. The land calls to some of us."

He lifted his hand to brush a tendril of hair away from her jaw. Warmth streamed through her and pooled between her thighs.

"What do you want for yourself, Chevy?" The urgency in his voice made her rock back. He hooked an arm under his head and stared up at her.

She nibbled her lower lip. She was rattled and her thoughts scattered. Slowly, she organized them into words. "When a woman gets to a certain age, there's a high expectation for her to get married and start a family, but I'm far from that. I'm leaving it up to my sister."

"You never want that for yourself?"

"I didn't say that. I don't exactly meet men with staying power." She nudged his shoulder playfully, but his face remained an unsmiling mask. She stumbled on, "I don't have to get

169

married to validate my life. I love working on my father's ranch. I do important work that I adore."

An image loomed in her mind's eye—Foster emerging from a barn on their own ranch, striding toward her, big muscles rolling, and scooping her into his arms. Taking her to bed—their bed.

She'd come here to remind herself she didn't need to fall into some stupid romance trap with a man who'd change in a heartbeat and act like the asshole he truly was. She didn't have enough time with Foster to know if he was a dick or not, but her gut said that he was genuine. Right now, with her.

Yes, being with him long-term was a silly, girlish dream but maybe it was time she came to terms with the fact that she wanted sex and sweet times like these with a man of her own. A man like Foster. And hell, she wanted romance too. She just hadn't found the right guy yet.

She loved being treated this way.

He took her hand in his and ran his thumb back and forth across her knuckles. She needed to remind herself this was fake.

Then why did the look in his eyes seem anything but?

"Foster..."

He pressed a kiss to her fingers, melting her. She leaned closer, and he coiled her in by her nape. Her breasts met his hard chest. He palmed her ass, drawing her fully atop him, naked from head to toe. Then he kissed her with such passion and sweet thoroughness that she was only left more confused as to what was real and what was make-believe.

* * * * *

"Hey, Fos."

He pivoted at the sound of his name. Lil strode toward him, grinning and happier than he'd seen her in weeks. "You finally got out of the office? I didn't hear someone else had been hired."

"Nah, I pushed Bastian behind the desk and ordered him to stay there."

Foster chuckled. "Bet he loves that. The only person I know who hates being locked inside more than you is him."

Her eyes twinkled. "I know." Then she sobered, studying him. "Something weighing on you?"

171

"You make a damn good manager even if you don't want the job."

"So something *is* weighing on you."

A couple broke from the barn, the female running as fast as she could, bare breasts cupped in her hands and laughter rippling behind her as the Boot Knocker chased her. Lil and Foster watched them go and then turned back to their conversation.

Lil gave a shake of her head. "Didn't think I'd ever get used to seeing naked couples run out of my daddy's barn, rest his soul, but it just happened. Now spill it, Fos."

He shifted his weight to the side and kicked at the spotty turf. "Need to get some seed on these bare spots."

"Don't change the subject." She grabbed him by the elbow and towed him to a log bench he'd made himself when he'd first come to the ranch. Once they were seated side-by-side, she said, "Is it trouble with your client?"

He contemplated her question. "Sorta. I don't feel like I make her happy."

"Seems happy to me. I saw her at breakfast."

"There's more to it."

She straightened and looked him in the eyes for a long minute. "Damn," she said under her breath.

"What?"

"I've been manager a few weeks and I'm already losing a man. Hugh warned me of this, and you're showing all the signs."

"Signs?"

"Of falling for your client. Shit, what am I going to do? If one of you falls, you all start dropping like the Texas guys, getting hooked up and leaving. Then I'll have to interview men and how will I know if they're right for their positions?"

He raised his brows at the question. "Try them on for size?" His mind reeled with her words, despite his joking.

Falling for Chevy?

It couldn't be possible, could it? Then again, Shayne had said something similar to him not two days before.

Foster turned inward, soul searching. Lil said all the signs were there, but how the hell did he even know what the signs were to find out if she was right?

He wanted to make Chevy happy above anything else. It kept him awake, thinking that he might be failing.

The thought of her leaving ripped him up.

Shit. She's right. I'm falling for my client.

How had it happened? Chevy was amazing, but what made her so different from the other women he'd been with here on the ranch, or hell, outside it for that matter? His life had been filled with females, and yet he couldn't see any beyond Chevy. It was like someone had planted a stop sign behind her and she was it for him.

Lil was going on, about how she couldn't try the Boot Knockers candidates on for size. She wasn't that woman, and Foster knew it, and on and on.

He pretended he was listening, but his mind was far away. Back on the side of that pond with Chevy in his arms. She made him better than any man he'd been before. He'd discovered some new inner peace, as if he'd found what he'd searched for his entire life. Until a few days ago, he'd believed that had been the ranch. Now he wasn't so sure.

She couldn't stay another week, but maybe he could persuade her to return in two weeks, after her sister's wedding shower.

He thought of the wedding and Chevy looking beautiful in a gown. Then he realized she'd probably have a date and he clamped his jaw so tight that his tendons creaked.

Something was definitely happening inside him. He couldn't quite put his finger on it yet, but he had to figure it out as fast as possible.

Chevy didn't have much time left on the ranch.

Chapter Nine

Chevy dismounted from the horse and looped the reins around her hand, guiding it toward the barn. "You're a good horse, aren't you? You deserve a nice rub-down and a bag of oats."

"And what do I get for being good?" Foster's warm words were at her ear. How had he sneaked up on her that way? She stifled a shiver at the heat he brought against her spine. "Where did you come from?"

"I was standing over there." He pointed past her and pressed a quick kiss to her cheek. "Leave the horse for a minute—it'll be all right. I want to show you somethin'."

Oh no.

Oh yes. Her body yearned for whatever he had to show her. She dropped the reins, and the horse didn't move from its spot, just dipped his head to crop the sparse grass.

Foster came around her and held her gaze for a heartbeat before taking her hand. He led her just inside the shadows of the barn.

She blinked, adjusting to the low lighting, and then heard a soft moan coming from her left. She turned her head and spotted what had made the noise.

It was no horse.

She went still as she realized what she was looking at. Two men sharing a woman. Her naked body a tawny brown, glistening with perspiration as she was passed between them. The cowboy with a black hat bent to her mouth, running his tongue over her lips with a flick that made her open to him.

Chevy's insides clutched with lust. Foster curled an arm around her middle, anchoring her to his chest. Together they stared at the sight.

As the cowboy kissed the slim brunette, the other was at her back, kissing her neck and down her spine to the crest of her buttocks. The woman moaned, and the cowboy at her front pulled her closer so she had to angle her back. This gave the man behind her access to her behind.

Oh God, Chevy wanted to whisper to Foster. Had she worn an expression like that when he licked and kissed her ass?

Her pussy squeezed, and juices soaked her panties. Foster's cock was iron-hard against her. She wiggled slightly to get closer to that rigid length, and he vibrated with a groan.

The cowboys spun the woman, trading places. They were shirtless, their jeans hanging open to reveal impressive bulges trapped behind cotton underwear. One bent to suck the brunette's peaked breasts and the cowboy in the black hat took up where the first had left off — at her ass.

"They're readying her for them," Foster murmured in her ear.

She glanced at the trio, wondering if they'd heard. But they seemed to be so involved in each other, they didn't realize she and Foster looked on or they didn't care. Would she ever get to that point?

Maybe. With Foster and Wyoming? A sliver of need sank between her thighs.

She wanted to ask what they were readying the woman for, but she knew. They were going to take her at the same time, and they needed her loosened to receive them both.

A dark moan filled the space as cowboy number two released her nipple and sank to his knees before her. "Hold her while I eat this sweet pussy," he commanded.

The cowboy in the black hat pinned her against his muscled front and the second man spread her thighs. He glanced up at her. "Such a beautiful pussy. I'm going to make it cum and then fuck it."

"And I'm going to finger you here." The cowboy in the black hat slipped a finger between her buttocks to settle over her anus. She whimpered. He placed his lips to her ear and said something Chevy couldn't hear, but she strained forward to try.

Foster held her tight, and she ground against him. He ground back, finding her breast with one big palm. Her nipple puckered under his touch, and she couldn't tear her gaze away from the ménage a trois if the barn went up in flames. Hell, with all the sexual tension here, it just might combust.

She throbbed for more as the two cowboys went at the brunette with a plan to fulfill their darkly-spoken promises. One tongued her pussy while the other sank his finger into her backside. She rocked between them in a state of ecstasy, her face more beautiful with each bit of pleasure she received.

When she cried out and jerked her hips forward, the man eating her pussy moaned. He

179

licked faster and then finally slowed. He raised his head, lips glistening with her juices.

Chevy was on the verge of coming too. If Foster didn't ease her, she'd blow up. She grabbed his hand and moved it from her aching nipples to her waist. He hummed with appreciation as he slid his hand down her jeans and into her panties. She was drenched, and he bit her earlobe.

"So fucking hot," he ground out in barely a murmur.

The couple had moved, both cowboys rolling on condoms. The man in the back hat lay back on a hay bale, and the other man positioned the woman over him. Lube was unearthed from some hiding spot and doused over the cowboy's cock, bouncing in the air.

"Sink down on top of me, baby. That's it." He groaned as she settled her ass over his shaft. If she'd taken a man here before, Chevy couldn't tell. But in a few downward thrusts, he filled her ass completely.

Chevy's own pucker clenched. Foster had made her come there before, and the memories fueled her need. She wanted him inside her, moving in that most forbidden spot.

The other cowboy pressed the woman back to lie with her back against her lover's chest. He wrapped her in his arms and kissed her neck while the other man nestled between her thighs.

She cried out as he pushed in.

"Fuck, I feel your cock inside her, Nolan."

"Feel yours too." The black-hatted cowboy grunted.

The woman was kissed and caressed until she relaxed, and then they started to move.

Foster worked his finger over Chevy's hard clit, stroking it back and forth and around and around until she went on tiptoe to get closer to his tormenting touch. She burned, wanted to be kissed and taken in all ways just as this lucky woman before her was. Which man did she belong to for the week? It didn't matter, because he was giving her everything right now.

With a start, Chevy realized that Foster wanted to do that for her. Give it all, every single sexual pleasure he could. Pressure escalated inside her. She rocked her hips to feel his hardness at her backside, and he jerked his hips to give her more sensation as he teased her clit.

"You want that, don't you, baby doll? To feel me and another man inside you, all linked."

She managed a nod, eyes glued to the scene. Both men moving in tandem, and then finding a new rhythm that strengthened the woman's cries. Her noises echoed off the high barn walls.

Chevy knew she was getting close, as was the brunette. Would it be weird to come along with her?

Yes, but so fucking hot.

She matched the woman's breathing as her own body climbed toward its pinnacle. Foster sucked on a spot on her throat while he drove her higher.

"Come for me," the cowboy fucking the woman's pussy said. "I feel you clamping down on me so tight."

"Her ass is contracting. She's about to explode." The cowboy in the black hat named Nolan issued a harsh groan that sent the female over the edge.

She came with a scream, and the cowboys pounded into her with a fierce need of their own.

Chevy's eyes rolled back in her head as her own release rushed her, swallowed her. Any noise she made was drowned by theirs.

And by Foster's groan as she came on his fingers.

* * * * *

Foster dragged Chevy outside away from the trio in the barn. He stuck his pussy-wet fingers in his mouth while tearing at his fly. He barely pulled it into his fist when Chevy dropped to her knees in front of him and swallowed him whole.

Shock and arousal tore through his senses as he found himself buried deep in his beautiful lover's throat. He cupped her head and dragged her closer until her sweet, pouty lips met his body. His cock head pulsated at the back of her throat.

"Fuck, I won't last two seconds in your hot mouth," he said on a growl.

"Mmm." She hummed around him, shooting him up another notch. He fisted her hair. Drove into her. She sucked, hollowing her cheek with strong pulls. Then she backed off and swirled her tongue up and down his

183

length. As she worked at the tip, he spilled pre-cum into her mouth.

She lapped it up and sucked him right to the root again. He threw his head back, seeing stars. Fuck, she'd been so responsive back there, watching his buddies fuck that woman. If she let him share her, he knew he'd give her something she'd never had. He wanted to be her first in all things, and sinking into her ass was one claim he was damn well staking.

His balls swung forward against her delicate chin, and he jerked his gaze back to her face. Her eyes open to watch him, her cheeks flushed. He tensed, and that dark need rose up from the base of his spine. Three more sucks, four... He burst with a groan, pouring his seed into her hot mouth.

She swallowed once but then let the rest run out of her lips, and he didn't give a damn what she did—it was perfect. She was perfect for him.

He cradled her jaw and focused on her eyes, which were hazy with passion. He dragged her up his body and kissed her with every ounce of his own desire, hoping she understood that he felt different with her, even if he couldn't—shouldn't—voice it.

* * * * *

The slanted back porch roof of the lodge was the perfect angle for lying and cloud-watching.

And for hiding.

Nobody would guess Chevy was up here, and that she wanted it that way. She needed time to herself. Even taking one of the horses meant she'd run into other couples and Foster could easily find her. But when she'd spotted a way to climb up far enough to hitch herself onto the roof, she'd seized the opportunity.

She stared at the thick clouds scudding across the sky until her eyes blurred. Sometimes she was so stupid, and this was one of those times. She liked Foster—a lot. More than she should.

Only somehow it felt different too. The guys from her past, she got this heady feeling like she'd been wound up like a mechanized toy and was about to be let loose. She was always wanting more, more, more with those men. She couldn't wait to see them again, to get that phone call or text.

With Foster, she still felt a certain giddiness but it was more of a drunken state. The second she set eyes on him, she was

185

buzzed. A feeling that didn't end in a hangover or regret, and that was damned confusing.

She wanted to hear about his experiences and thoughts on the ranch, while with the other men she'd dated, she couldn't wait to hear more about how into her he was.

"I wanted the bullshit," she said aloud, in awe of her self-discovery.

She closed her eyes to shut out the clouds, the world, Foster. But that was easier said than done. The man swam through her mind in that lazy backstroke from the pond, all powerful muscles slicing through the water with the ease of a great white shark.

He'd undergone a change recently too. Whether he was growing more comfortable in her presence or something else, she had no guess. She only knew that when he'd looked at her outside the barn, her heart had leaped.

Higher and faster than she'd ever felt before.

For once, she was more afraid of her emotions than ever too. She was finally, truly, completely falling for a man, and he was a gigolo who serviced women.

Her imagination ran rampant for a minute, to taking him home with her, introducing him to her parents. Her daddy'd like him straightaway, and her momma would smile knowingly, as she had with Michael and her sister.

Chevy daydreamed about working alongside him and then finding ease in each other's arms after a long day.

She snapped herself out of it as she heard the scraping of something near the right support of the porch. She sat up and looked at the corner just as a cowboy hat popped over the rim.

Two eyes blazing with mischief.

"Knew I'd find you up here." Foster's biceps bulged as he did a pull-up.

She shook her head. How a big body like that moved with such effortless grace was beyond her.

"How would you know I'm up here?"

"Guessed you'd search out the quietest, most isolated spot you could."

"So you thought of the roof? No way. You must have seen me come up here. Or somebody else did."

"Nope." He crab-walked up the low slope to settle beside her. Suddenly, the sun seemed so much hotter. She broke out in a dew of sweat. When he eyed her, dammit if her heart didn't kick into a flutter.

His bad-boy smile turned her inside out. "I mighta seen a barn cat giving you away, though."

"A—" She broke off, remembering the gray cat that had circled her legs right before she'd climbed onto the roof.

"Cat was sitting down there looking upward, and as I couldn't see a bird's nest, I figured it was waiting for someone to come back down and pet it."

"Damn traitorous cat."

He grinned, teeth white and straight and blinding to her heart. She was more than just falling for Foster—she was opening her heart to him. Something she never had with those other guys despite what she'd believed.

"Do you want me to go?" he asked, low.

She loved his solid strength next to her. Loved seeing his smile and twinkling eyes. The way he tugged his hat low and slightly crooked.

She shook her head.

"Good." He lay back and held out his arms. She couldn't stop herself from resting her head in that hollow of his chest where she fit so perfectly and letting him mesh their hands.

Hands that looked beautiful together. Hard-working hands, both of them. They could do so much together. Live, work, love.

She swallowed hard.

"Mighty fine spot to make out. Wanna try?" He ran his nose back and forth over her temple.

His light, masculine scent fogged her mind, set her on fire. She definitely wanted to make out, to kiss and grope each other until they couldn't wait another minute and he'd take her right here, with the sky above them and nothing else that mattered much.

But she had to put a stop to this before her poor heart cracked in half and he buried himself deep inside it. She'd have no hope of evicting him then.

"Is that all you think about? Sex?"

He used his knuckles under her jaw to tilt her face and look at her. His eyes were very serious, his lips set in a line. "What's really going on, Chevy? Why'd you escape?"

"I just needed to think." She didn't meet his gaze but stared at his upper lip. So hard-looking but soft against hers. And all over her body.

"You needed to be kissed in a spot as beautiful as you." He started moving in for that kiss, but she stopped him.

"Can you ever not talk like that?" She was being unfair, because he said plenty. "Just be plain with me."

"Okay, fine." He drawled out the last word, slow and soft. Goosebumps raised on her arms. "The cat did give you away, but I come up here too, sometimes. To think. Actually, I was up here this morning after leaving your bed."

She felt like a live wire, and one touch would send her an electrified frenzy. She waited.

"I needed time to consider why I want you to stay with me another week. Two weeks, hell months." He searched her eyes, and if the world ended right now, she couldn't look away from his steady, solemn stare. "I feel different with you, Chevy. You make me want to get up in the morning and go to sleep at night making you happy, and that is above and beyond a Boot Knocker's duty."

Damn her tripping heart.

"I think I'm falling for you. My friends think so too."

"You've… discussed this with others?"

He nodded.

Shock froze her in place for a moment. Then in a flurry, she scrambled down the roof to the edge.

"Chevy, wait."

She couldn't. She needed a new thinking spot, but she had a feeling every place she tried to hide, she'd never escape the man who was filling her mind, heart and soul so completely.

She dangled her feet toward the ground until she found the spot that had helped her climb up. Sure enough, the cat was there. It gave a loud meow when she landed next to it.

"Sorry, cat. I'll pet you next time." She took off toward the cabin as fast as her legs could carry her. She hoped Foster would take the hint and leave her alone.

Hell, who was she kidding? She wanted him to throw open that door and tell her more about how he felt and she would finally admit that she felt the same.

"You coming to the strip corn-hole tournament tonight, Foster?" The rhythm of Shayne's shovel in the earth had soothed Foster for a spell, and his buddy knew something was eating at him enough to stay quiet. It seemed they were going to have a conversation now.

"Dunno. Maybe." Foster concentrated on his task. It seemed the paddock was forever filling with water on one corner when it rained, and they'd gotten a doozy of a summer storm earlier.

Foster's first instinct was to go to Cabin 3 and wind his arms around Chevy, to find a way to pass the time during the power outage from the storm. But he'd reached the door in the height of the downpour and found it locked.

He hadn't knocked or gone in search of a key. He could take a hint.

He and Shayne had ended up here, shoveling a ditch to drain the water and up to their ankles in muck.

"Field out back of the lodge will still be dry enough for it," Shayne went on.

Foster grunted.

Shayne set his shovel in the earth and leaned on it to stare at him. "What's going on?"

He looked up and met his friend's gaze. If he could confide in anyone, it was him.

"I fucked up."

"How so?"

But Foster didn't know how to form the words to say he'd bared himself to Chevy and she'd run away, locked him out. A woman in her situation *would* do that, he kept telling himself. She'd been given lines of bullshit from men and was wary. Didn't mean it hurt Foster any less.

"Talk it out, bro." Shayne wasn't moving that shovel an inch despite the water that needed draining.

Foster set down his own shovel hard. The blade sank deep into the mud, and he tore off his hat. "Jesus, what am I thinking? I've had a lot of pussy, but she's more than that. If I met her anywhere but here, I'd follow her around just to get her attention."

"That's called stalking."

Foster leveled his gaze at him. "You know what I mean, ya ass."

"Yeah, I do." Shayne tucked his chin down. "I had that once."

"What'd you do about it?"

"I left and came here. Never let it take root."

"Fuck. Now what do I do?" Foster felt more riled than a bull-rider on a dud bull that just sat there in the middle of the arena. He felt stuck with no hope of winning.

He pushed out all the air in his lungs and forgot how to fill them again for a second. Finally, he sucked in a harsh gasp.

"Only you can answer that question, Fos. Or maybe she can."

Foster stared at him for a full minute before he realized what he needed to do. "I gotta find Wyoming." He walked away from the paddock, leaving the shovel upright in the mud.

Damn straight. I'm going to get some answers. Or some response besides her running away.

He'd stalled out in getting Chevy to realize how serious he was. Well, he and Wyoming could be pretty damn persuasive—all night long.

He headed for the office. Lil looked up as the door slammed behind him. She took one look at his face and stood up. "Oh shit. It's happening, isn't it?"

"What's happening?"

"You're leaving."

He shook his head. "I need into the cabinet."

"*The* cabinet?"

"Yup. Where's the key?"

They kept all the new dildos and bondage toys locked up in a cabinet. The office manager was in charge of them, doling them out as needed.

"What do you need from it?" She wet her lower lip nervously, and he gave her a second glance.

"Silk ropes and a vibe. Maybe a coupla other things if I see them."

"Okay." She bit her lower lip and skirted the desk. He followed her swaying ass to the back of the office where the floor-to-ceiling closet was. She fumbled for the key and fitted it into the lock, hesitating before turning it.

There was definitely something going on.

"Lil? I don't have all day."

"Oh. Yes. Here you go." She twisted the key and swung open the door.

He stepped up to it and opened both doors wide. The contents looked strange, like there was a lot of inventory missing. Dildos in particular.

He pivoted to her with raised eyebrows.

"Shut up. I'll replace them all as soon as the shipment arrives."

"Having some good evenings, I'm guessing."

She flushed to the roots of her hair, and perspiration broke out on her forehead. He'd laugh at her discomposure if he wasn't battling to keep his cool over Chevy.

"No judgment, Lil."

"A woman has needs."

"Needs for thirty vibrators, I guess. I'll take these." He reached in and took a coil of black rope braided from satin and a small clitoral vibrator that obviously hadn't seemed worth Lil's attention.

He squeezed her shoulder on the way past her. "Any idea where I'd find Wyoming?"

"Think he's ridin' the ridge, checking on the young'uns."

"Thanks."

"Wait—aren't you supposed to be working on the flood in the paddock?"

"Shayne's got it covered. See ya, Lil." He strode out of the office and went for the barn. He needed a horse to reach Wyoming quick.

Chapter Ten

With a towel clutched around her damp body, Chevy stepped into the bedroom and stopped dead.

She looked between the two big cowboys leaning in various enticing positions. Foster in a relaxed pose against the bedroom doorframe and Wyoming with a hip against the dresser and his arms crossed nonchalantly. As if they waited to ambush a woman wearing only a towel every day.

They probably do.

A thrill like she was on a roller coaster lifted her heart. "What's this?"

Like she didn't know. Like she hadn't been gagging for this moment since finding out Foster shared his women.

A crooked smile cut across Foster's handsome face, lending him a roguish look. He pulled away from the doorway, thigh muscles bulging with the action.

She glanced lower. Something else was bulging too. She flicked a look at Wyoming and found him sporting an erection too.

Shit. Could she handle this? They wouldn't even fit inside her.

Could she walk away and always wonder what it was like to be with two men?

She sucked her lower lip into her mouth. The towel almost slipped out of her grasp, and two grins spread over her as the men noticed.

"Might as well drop it, sweet stuff. Show us what you've got under that thin terrycloth." Damn, Wyoming knew how to send a woman into a tither. A flush climbed her throat and settled in her cheeks. Suddenly, she worried that Foster would mind another man flirting with her.

No, she was being dumb. It wasn't like he was her boyfriend.

Still, she turned her gaze his way only to find his eyes burning with lust.

He liked her being the center of another man's desires. Twisted as it was, warmth flooded her. Only a very confident man could allow that, whether she was his for a week or forever.

"Maybe we should start things off. What do ya say, Wyoming?"

Wyoming was as tall as Foster with broad shoulders and a slightly thicker body rimmed with muscle. He pulled off his hat, revealing mussed brown hair, not as dark as Foster's but the color of rich Guinness.

Chevy had no idea what to do in a situation like this. Nobody had ever taught her manners when two men started making out in her room on a sex ranch. But that's exactly what Foster and Wyoming did.

They stepped up to each other and kissed as if it was the most natural thing in the world. For them, it probably was.

And it was hot as fucking Hades. Lawdy, her nipples couldn't get harder. A bead of wetness slipped down her bare inner thigh.

They brushed their lips lightly over each other's. Then Foster gripped Wyoming around the back of the neck and yanked him in to deepen the kiss.

A noise broke from Chevy. God, they were all angular jaws sporting five o'clock shadows and tense muscles. She didn't know where to look first. The way their biceps strained against their shirts looked mighty pretty. But the bump of their groins, bulge to bulging cock, made her quiver.

She bit back another noise as they began to move against each other. Slow grinding movements that pulled a groan and a growl from the men. She didn't know who made which sound, and she stopped caring.

Wyoming yanked Foster's shirt over his head and bent to his nipple. The small brown nub in the middle of his hard pec was something Chevy'd worked over quite often, because she loved how turned on he got.

Seemed Wyoming knew this about her lover too. Which strangely made her feel instantly closer to the unknown cowboy. They both knew how to pleasure Foster. They could work him over good.

She watched Foster's eyelids flutter as Wyoming took his nipple between his teeth and worried it back and forth. He ended the torment with a flip of his tongue, and Foster thrust his cock against his buddy.

They shared a grin and then Foster removed Wyoming's shirt. When she saw the carved planes of the man's back, she sucked in a gasp. He looked like a bodybuilder. So much flesh to score with her nails.

She was slippery as hell, ready to join in. But she hadn't been invited yet and she wasn't going to miss the show. She forgot about holding her towel so tightly and it slipped a bit to reveal the top of one breast.

Foster reached for Wyoming's nipples. With a start, she realized they were both pierced. He tugged at the silver hoops and the man issued a harsh noise.

"Maybe I should lead you around by these," Foster rasped.

"I'll fucking follow you anywhere if you do. It feels amazing." He ran his hand down the ridges of Foster's abs to his belt.

Chevy locked her sights on the maneuver, because she was panting to see them touch each other's cocks. And more.

Would they suck each other off? Fuck each other?

When had she become such a depraved woman? She didn't give a damn, though. She had a personal porn going on in front of her, and one thing she'd learned at the ranch was how much she loved watching.

No surprise that Wyoming knew how to navigate a man's clothes. But what did make Chevy's eyes open wider was how well he knew Foster's body. He had his jeans open and his cock in hand in seconds.

Foster looked into Wyoming's eyes. "Suck me."

"Thought you'd never ask." He dropped to his knees.

A whimper left her and Foster swung his gaze away from the man's lips poised at his swollen head to her. A dark jolt of electricity had her clenching her fists. That look Foster wore… It was almost as though he was saying, *This is all for you. He's sucking my cock so you can watch.*

How fucked up was that? She didn't know where to look—at the pleasure crossing Foster's face or Wyoming parting his lips to swallow his cock.

In the end, she looked between both, sometimes rapid-fire. Taking it all in, drinking it up so she could use it later in her fantasies.

Wyoming's cheek hollowed as he sucked the length right to the root. Foster steadied himself with his hands on his lover's shoulders and alternated between watching him and staring deeply into Chevy's eyes.

When Wyoming cupped his balls and began to lightly fondle them, Foster tightened his jaw.

He was getting too aroused. He was going to break it off soon.

As soon as she thought this, he pushed back. Wyoming caught his cock in his fist and pumped it five times before Foster finally said, "Enough."

They turned to her as one. Wyoming drew to his feet and they approached. She forgot about holding her towel and it fluttered to the floor, revealing her nudity.

"You lied, Fos. She's more fucking beautiful than you said."

"Hard to describe perfection." Foster reached her first. With an arm around her middle, he drew her against him. She gasped as her nipples met his hot bare chest. And his thick cock ground into her lower belly.

Need shattered her self-control and she kissed him. As he explored her with his tongue, she realized there were too many hands on her. She couldn't concentrate on which belonged to whom. Her side, her breast, her buttocks, her inner thigh. She shuddered with pleasure at the heightened awareness unlike anything she'd ever had.

Then Foster broke the kiss and another mouth claimed hers. Warm, hard, unfamiliar but tasting of mint and musk. She didn't give into him the way she had Foster, but he wasn't giving up on her. Wyoming tugged her against him, letting her learn his hardness and steely erection too.

Foster trailed kisses down her throat to her breasts. Wyoming moved from the kiss and downward to suck her nipple into his mouth at the same moment Foster did.

She quaked. Strong pulls on her breasts made her pussy grip with need. She flooded her inner thighs. Passion rose up and she had no idea where to direct the energy. In the end, she clutched both men and guided them over her nipples and breasts.

"Get her on the bed," Foster grated out.

They lifted her and spread her open, each man holding a thigh. Oh God, they weren't going to lick her pussy together, were they?

She didn't know if she'd survive it.

Wyoming bit her inner thigh, making her cry out.

"Not fair. I get to leave a mark too," Foster said, biting into her flesh.

Harsh breaths broke from her as they kissed and licked down her thighs to her very center.

Yes, they're definitely licking my pussy together.

Two tongues slipped up and down her soaking wet folds. The sensation was... mind-blowing. She couldn't think, only feel. So hot, driving her higher. Swirling up and down, trapping her clit between their tongues.

"Oh my God. Yes," she cried out.

Foster's arm bulged and she realized he was stroking his stiff cock. The idea turned her on even more. Two men were sharing her, tasting her together. And it was the most erotic experience she could ever imagine.

She had a feeling there was more to come.

Wyoming sucked her clit while Foster tongue-fucked her pussy. Long seconds passed and her leg muscles trembled as her insides clenched and released. She started to burn, but they moved in unison and met again. Licking up and down, up and down. One finger speared her pussy deep, and she screamed.

She had no idea who was fingering her, didn't care. Then someone added a finger to her backside. She had no hope of lasting — she came on a searing cry.

* * * * *

Foster burned to slide into Chevy's hot, tight pussy but there was much more for his cowgirl. Hell, he hadn't even broken out the silk rope and vibe yet. When he and Wyoming finished with her, she wasn't going to be able to walk. If she was even conscious.

Wyoming lapped at her creamy slit and moaned. Foster loved seeing him enjoy his woman as much as he did.

My woman.

How it had happened was anybody's guess, and he'd spent enough time in his life over-analyzing things. He didn't care how but she was his. He was freaking falling for her. Probably already had fallen, was too far gone to stop now.

He kissed a path up her body to her lips. She gasped and threw herself into the moment. She liked tasting herself, and his cock was bursting now.

"I can't stop licking this beautiful pussy," Wyoming said.

"Get her nice and wet for us. Loosen her. She has to be loose to fit us both."

Chevy moaned, and Foster smiled down at her. She leaned upward and bit his bottom lip.

Damn, the sting, the urgency inside her— he unleashed a growl and slammed his lips over hers. The kiss turned brutal, all-consuming. She was so right for him from the tip of her cowgirl hat to the toes of her worn boots. Her sexy body was a bonus, because it was her mind he was really drawn to, like a bee to honey. If he had his way, he'd come back for more and more. Hopefully she'd realize this was right for them. His idea to see her after the wedding shower had to be realized or he'd lose his mind with wanting.

He slowed the kiss as she stiffened. Wyoming was going to make her come on his tongue, and Foster wanted to watch.

Leaning back, he fixed his gaze on the erotic sight of another man licking her. He rasped his beard scruff over her pussy and sucked on her clit. Her stomach dipped and she stopped breathing.

Foster reached out and stroked her hard nipples softly. She rocked her hips upward and came.

They brought her down slowly together, kissing, caressing. Foster reached for the condoms and then stood to shuck off all his clothing. Wyoming saw him hold up that condom and the twinkle in his eye and did the same with rapid speed.

On the bed, Chevy lay sprawled, eyes half-lidded after her orgasms. Foster slid the condom to the base of his cock with one hard flick of his wrist. "Get over her and let her suck your cock. Chevy?"

Her eyes widened and then a look of pure hunger claimed her pretty features. She nodded, and Wyoming took a moment to kiss her deeply. Then he hovered over her, his cock at her lips. She didn't hesitate and sucked him straight in.

Wyoming groaned. Foster didn't wait either—he pushed into Wyoming's ass.

He met little resistance and in seconds was buried balls-deep. He knew about now that the man he was fucking should be streaming pre-cum. He wished he could see Chevy swallowing around it, her throat working as she pleasured him with her sweet mouth.

Damn, she was good at everything she did, and so far she was a pro at taking two men. Foster withdrew, and they all made a noise of surrender. Then he pumped back in with two short thrusts.

"Fuuuuck," Wyoming grated out.

Foster gripped him by the hip and anchored himself deeper. The insane tight warmth enveloped him, made his nuts pound for release. But he couldn't. That was for Chevy. He'd only cum in her ass, and this was just a warm-up.

Knowing he could only take Wyoming to the brink too, he slowed his pace and then finally pulled out.

Wyoming continued to fuck into Chevy's mouth a few more times before he found the self-control to stop. He rolled away from her, and Foster found her staring at his cock.

"I love fucking ass, doesn't matter if it's a man or yours. Right now it's your turn." Foster held her gaze as he discarded the used condom and donned another.

She ran her tongue over her lips, swollen from sucking.

Wyoming gathered her up against his chest while Foster stretched on the bed beneath her. "Don't worry, we'll use plenty of lube and take it slow, sweet stuff."

As soon as Chevy's sleek body covered his, Foster was ready. He needed inside her—now. Needed to feel her come apart between them.

"Okay?" he whispered into her ear. She nodded and he found the full tube of lube under the pillow where he'd hidden it. He oiled his fingertips and slid them between her buttocks. Smoothing it over and over until she started to quiver. Then he added more oil and worked his finger into her ass. One and then two. He stopped there because he didn't have the stamina, and he could see Wyoming's cock about to burst, ridged with veins and the head purple.

He dumped a copious amount onto his cock and drizzled more over her pucker. "Sit back on it, baby doll. Fuck!" He hadn't expected her to go at it so quickly, but she did, thrusting herself down so the head popped right in. The worst was over, and she seemed no worse for wear.

In fact, her neck was arched, and she was rasping a throaty moan.

"Bear down and take me all the way. That's it." She dropped over him in one long glide. Every inch of his cock filled her tight, sweet ass. Electric heat filtered through his system. He ached to pound up into her, but he had to make this right, take it slow.

Wyoming positioned his rubbered cock at the V of her legs. "Spread wider. Like that." He groaned as he nestled at her wet opening.

"You all right, baby doll?" Foster asked.

"Soo good," she said with a shiver.

His balls clenched, and he met Wyoming's gaze. The man pushed in. Inch by slow inch until Foster felt her body stretched full and the pressure of the other man's cock against his through the thin barrier of her body.

Dark need made Foster's head swirl. He bit lightly into her throat as she lay down in his arms completely, splayed open and pinioned on two cocks.

"I..."

Foster's concern was only for her. "What is it?"

"Need to move." She heaved upward on his cock as Wyoming moved too. Withdrawing, sinking in again. All three of them moving like they'd done this a hundred times. And they would do it again, he guaranteed it—if she came back to the ranch.

He had to see more of her. Letting this go wasn't an option.

Wyoming kissed her, the tangling of tongues driving Foster's need up another notch. He was crazed with it. Lust stole his sanity.

"Oh fuck, she's tightening on my cock." Wyoming sounded as if he'd run a mile.

Foster focused on her ass, a tight clench around his own cock. Sure enough, small pulsations were starting in her. She was rising. And so was he.

He sucked her throat and whispered hot words to her. Then he grabbed Wyoming and kissed him. The taste of him—man and pussy—sent him over the edge. He hadn't wanted to come first, but it was too late for that. The first jet left his body.

* * * * *

"I'm coming," she cried, curling in on the ecstasy that had her in its clutches. Her pussy squeezed so tight even as her ass clamped down around the other cock filling her. She was stretched beyond imagination, the pressure building. "Please," she heard herself rasp. "Please let me come."

Wyoming pushed deep and Foster was still moving, the warmth of his release sending her into the dizzying realm of pleasure she craved.

Her scream echoed off the walls. Foster added another guttural groan. Then Wyoming began to pulse into her. They were so deep she had no idea where they started and she stopped. No walls seemed to separate them.

213

Yet when Wyoming slowly rolled off her, she knew where her true feelings lay — with the man underneath her, the one who was still buried in her ass.

He pumped one more time and found her clit, pressing it down into her body. She didn't think she could come again, but every touch was amplified and she did.

After that, she had no recollection of how she ended up lying between two strong cowboys, their arms wound around her and their lips moving over her skin again. But she wasn't going to complain. Not in the least. There were *hours* left in the day to seek more pleasure, and she wasn't going to waste a single one of them.

Hell, there are days left. We can stay in bed the whole time.

Then came the most embarrassing sound. Chevy jerked upright, mortified.

All three of them stared at the floor and her abandoned jeans.

A snicker came from Foster. "Is that Justin Bieber?"

She dived over the side of the bed, as bare as a porn star, which must have given the men an interesting view. She scrambled over to the pile of clothes she'd dropped before getting in the shower and located her phone after finding the wrong pocket—twice.

By then Justin's voice had cut off, thank the Lord and all the baby angels. But it took up ringing again almost immediately.

She popped to her feet. Her cowboy lovers lay grinning back at her. Heat scorched her face, and she felt sweat break out on her brow. It didn't help when their grins widened.

"No shame in liking the Bieb, baby doll."

"It's my sister's ringtone. I'll just..." She ducked into the bathroom and slammed the door to sounds of laughter from the men. She thumbed the button to take the call and leaned against the door with a *thump*.

"Sadie, what the hell?"

"Well hello to you, dear sister. What's put the bee up your ass?"

"The ringtone," she whispered furiously into the phone, imagining what the men must be discussing about her right this instant.

Naked.

Lying close to each other.

Damn, now her nipples were hard.

"What's wrong with the ringtone? It's our song," Sadie said.

It had been a joke at first, listening to the particular song together after one of Chevy's stupid breakups. Since then, it had become a sort of anthem for sisterhood. Around her family, she wasn't embarrassed in the least, but now Foster thought she was a fangirl.

She ran her fingers through her hair and focused on her sister. "What's up, anyway? Everything okay at home?"

"Yes, it's fine. Except one tiny thing."

"What's that?"

"The venue for the wedding shower's out."

Chevy gasped. She'd fucked up a lot in her life, and she wasn't fucking up her sister's special day. "Christ on a bucking bull, Sadie. Say you're joking."

"Would I joke about this? I'm freaked out, Michael's freaking out, Momma's paced a hole in the kitchen floor and Daddy's pissed he has to replace the worn portion now. I'm as serious as a murder of crows."

Chevy closed her eyes and counted to ten. They needed a new venue, and quick. That wouldn't be such a big deal except her sister had chosen wedding season to get married, and their small town sported exactly one fancy restaurant with an event room, a firehall and a church hall. There weren't any options left.

"We can fancy up the house."

"Sure, that'll be great—for our side of the family. Michael's got twelve aunts and what was the count? Twenty-nine cousins?"

"Okay, then outdoors."

"You can't count on the weather in Montana, sis. You know that. Keep talkin'."

"Shit, I don't know. Maybe the high school cafeteria would work. Set up long lunchroom tables and serve everything on those plastic trays…"

"Jesus, Chevy. You wait till it's your turn to get married. I'll have your wedding shower at the funeral parlor. But I know you're smart and you'll think of something. You've got a few more days."

Chevy opened her mouth to speak but her sister cut her off.

"Oh, and how's it going with the cowboy?" Sadie had lowered her voice as if they were talking about sex in church.

Unexpectedly, her eyes filled with tears. Whether it was the worry over having a special event for her sister or the truth of her own emotions, Chevy needed to talk. She slid down the door and hissed when her bare buttocks hit the cold tile.

In a whisper, she said, "It's good, Sadie."

"Uh-oh. Good means more coming from you."

She bowed her head and a single tear trickled from the corner of her eye. Her sister could always pull her real dilemmas right to the surface, and there was no pretending that Chevy wasn't falling for the cowboy she'd hired to help her stop being a pushover with men.

"Your plan backfired, didn't it?" Sadie's words were more shocking than the Bieber song after a burning-hot ménage a trois with two sexy cowboys.

Her throat worked. "It did."

"Oh Chevy."

"I'm a hopeless case." She sucked in a breath to fortify herself. "How did you know Michael was the one?"

"You're thinking the guy you're with might be? You've said that about how many other—"

"Just answer me."

A breathy sigh sounded through the line. "When I look at Michael, there's this thing. More than chemistry. Do you have that?"

She was already nodding. "Go on."

"And he didn't try to overly impress me with fake things. He found out I like to ride and he hooked up his horse trailer and took me to a new spot in the mountains. We had a wonderful day."

"I remember," she said miserably.

Hadn't Foster done that too? He'd dropped the dinner by moonlight right quick and taken her to that beautiful spot in the trees where they'd ended up winding their bodies around each other and cloud-gazing.

It could still be an act. He was well-trained for his job.

But her aching heart leaped with hope.

"I love waking up next to him. Sometimes I find him staring at me with this wonder on his face," her sister went on.

Oh God. Last time she'd awakened next to Foster, it had been to his dark eyes burning into her.

"What is going on up there, Chevy? Talk to me about it and I'll tell you if I think it could be the real deal."

219

"Later. I have to go." Before she let her mind skip wildly all over the hills of revelation.

Chevy'd fallen for Foster. For a man she'd only be with a few more days. She could calculate the number of seconds they had left together.

"I'll find a solution for the shower, okay? Don't call again. I don't want to hear the ringtone while I'm here."

Her sister giggled, damn her cute little soul to hell. "Okay. Call if you need me, sissy."

She hung up and leaned her head back against the door for the count of twenty heartbeats. The other room was completely quiet. She prayed they couldn't hear her conversation. She'd never be able to face them.

She opened the door and peeked in.

Nope—they definitely wouldn't have heard her. Not when they were so engrossed with each other.

The men were sixty-nining.

She drifted to her feet, her gaze locked on the sight of all that tanned, glistening muscle entwined in the most graceful pose she'd ever seen from anyone other than athletes.

Foster hovered over his lover, pumping his hips and his thick cock disappearing in and out of Wyoming's mouth. Meanwhile, his own lips were wrapped around the man's shaft, his eyes closed.

Chevy stood there another moment admiring what she was seeing and throbbing for more.

She stepped toward the bed and cupped her breasts in her palms. "It's time you take care of me now, boys."

Chapter Eleven

Chevy's head rested on Foster's biceps, her hair trailing over the sheets. He traced lazy circles on her stomach and listened to her slow breathing.

After Wyoming had slipped out, saying someone needed to work on the ranch, Foster and Chevy had turned to each other once more. Those moments alone... They'd undone him.

He couldn't let her walk away—not yet. He'd spent the last ten minutes rehearsing how he'd explain to Lil that this woman was a special case, that he hadn't done his job and he needed more time.

"It was my sister on the phone." Her voice startled him from his thoughts—he'd thought her dozing.

He flattened his palm on her stomach, letting her silken warmth radiate through his arm. "Everything all right?"

He could tell how strongly she was bonded to her sister by the few comments she'd made about her. How important it was to her to throw an amazing wedding shower proved it.

"Everything's all wrong. The shower venue is double-booked or something and now we have nowhere to throw it. I've been thinking about it for hours and can't come up with a place to hold it besides the barn. And that would take a lot of work to get it ready."

"Hold up." He leaned on one elbow to stare down at her. "You were thinking about a wedding shower when I was making you come?"

She nibbled her lower lip, holding back the smile he saw in her beautiful eyes. "Of course not. In between."

"Surrrre," he drawled.

She slapped him lightly. "I can hardly remember my name when you're with me. I surely couldn't be going over plans like that."

"My ego is intact now. Thank you." He ducked to bite her earlobe, and she wiggled against him. A slow stirring in his groin testified he wasn't done with her. Not after most of a day in bed. Certainly not after a week.

A thought hit.

She blinked up at him. A crinkle appeared between her eyes. "What's wrong?"

"Hold the shower here."

"What?" She pushed into a sitting position and he did too. Her hair was rumpled, and God, she looked cute as hell. He wanted to tumble her back into the sheets and not surface for another hour. His thoughts on the wedding shower would hold till then.

He reached for her.

She threw up her hands against his chest. "Uh-uh, Mr. Boot Knocker. Tell me what's going on in your mind."

"We have the lodge. It's big enough to hold a huge wedding party plus a football team or two."

She blinked at him, and he got distracted by her long lashes. So when she punched him in the arm, he started. "What was that for?"

"You weren't listening."

"How do you know? I was looking at you, wasn't I?"

"It's the way you were looking at me. We couldn't hold it here. It's unseemly."

"We'll keep everyone from fucking in the corners if that's what you're worried about."

"It *is* what I'm worried about. And all the women who wouldn't understand why people would come here for…"

He waggled his brows and rubbed a hand over his chest. "For a piece of this?"

"I'm going to punch you again."

He laughed and captured her hands to keep her from making good on her threat. "It's a ranch first and foremost, Chevy."

"Anybody could look up the location and see what else takes place here." She shook her head. "No."

He looked into her eyes and rubbed his thumbs over hers. "It would bring you back to me."

"What?" Her voice was a harsh whisper.

Before his mind booted up and overrode his emotions, he said, "I want you here with me. I don't want you to leave at all, but I'm willing to let you go for a few days before you come back for the shower. Then you can stay on until the weddin'."

"What are you saying?" Her words were barely audible and she searched his eyes.

"I'm feeling more for you, Chevy."

Her jaw dropped. She shook her head hard. "No."

"Yes. I've never felt this for anybody, let alone a client. It's different. You're different."

"You don't know me." She jerked her hands from his grasp.

"I know enough. I can't wait to learn more."

"What can you possibly have learned about me besides where to put your dick?"

"I do know that pretty damn well, but it's the little things. The way you look so happy and carefree when you're on the ranch. That you take two creams in your coffee and can peel an entire orange without breaking the peel."

"You could learn that just by having breakfast with me."

"Maybe, but there's more and you know it. You feel it too." He grabbed her by the shoulders so she couldn't bolt. She was close to it. Hell, his heart was hammering like a runaway horse's. Everything inside him bucked the idea of falling in love.

But with Chevy, the idea of her leaving and not knowing it was infinitely worse.

"Please. Look at me."

"Foster, this isn't real."

"It is on my end. Look me in the eyes and tell me you've been pretending to like me. Pretending that you aren't feeling the same."

His voice broke like a teen going through puberty.

"What about your job? Your clients?"

"How could I touch another woman now?"

"Oh Foster."

He cupped her jaw, so delicate under his fingers. Her eyes glowed, and he knew she was mirroring the same look he was giving her.

"I don't totally understand what's going on between us, but how can we ignore it? If we walk away and give up on it, then it's damn tragic. Won't you always wonder what if?"

After a second, she nodded.

He let go of her face and crushed her to his chest. "Stick around a little longer, Chevy. Stay on and make plans for the shower. Lil can help you with everything. Then you can help out on the ranch. We'll appreciate having you around."

She pushed away from his chest to look at him. "You mean you will appreciate me in your bed."

"That too. Don't fight it anymore, baby doll. I see you softening toward it already." He cupped her breast and smoothed his thumb over her nipple until it hardened at his touch.

"I don't know what I'm feeling, Foster."

"Aroused."

"Well yeah."

"Excited."

A sigh. "That too."

"Unsure that you're not just falling into the same old trap with a man who wants to suck you dry of emotions and then leave you."

She shuddered and buried her face against his chest again. "How do you know?"

He kissed the top of her head. "Because there's more to us. Believe me, it came as a surprise to me too. But now that it's out in the open, all I feel is excitement to learn it all. Don't you feel the same?"

* * * * *

Honestly, she felt like she was going to explode with joy. Or get up and run. Or fart. She was all bottled up. Any way she looked at it, this was all new to her.

Could she possibly have come to The Boot Knockers Ranch to become a stronger version of herself and end up falling harder than ever before? Somehow, none of that made her feel weak.

She was bold and strong, but she liked to be shown she was a woman with the little things. This week Foster had given her that. He enhanced her strengths and enjoyed them. If she'd suggested the sheep would naturally drive the elk back down the mountain, any of her old boyfriends would have told her to sit and relax while he took care of it.

Foster *was* different.

Even his suggestion that she throw the shower here was great. It solved her problem without taking over and telling her how to do it. She and Foster made a great team.

He'd asked her to ride out with him to give Wyoming a hand this morning, but she'd declined, saying she had things to think about and a shower to plan.

She sat at the small table for two in the corner of the lodge. Tall windows overlooked the ranch, showcasing the lush green and mountains. Yes, this would be the perfect space for Sadie's special day.

She'd had her sister email her a guest list and their addresses. If the ranch was hopelessly too far away for the majority of people, it wasn't a good idea after all. But as she glanced down the list, she grew more excited.

What do you have up your sleeve, big sister? The text came in from Sadie, and she smiled to herself.

I have a venue if you're open to excitement, she texted back.

Oh lord. I'm not sure if I like what you're about to say.

Chevy chuckled again.

Suddenly a body plopped into the seat across from her. She glanced up to see Lil. The woman set a coffee mug on the table and smiled. "You're as pretty as Foster said."

Chevy leaned back in surprise. "Th-thank you." Foster had spoken of her to Lil?

"Don't look so shocked. I know everything that goes on here. Not that I want to. I'd rather be in the fields." She turned her head to stare longingly out the window at the land that belonged to her.

"I bet you miss it."

Lil met Chevy's gaze. "I do. I hope the Texas people find me a replacement office manager quick. I'm not cut out to be stuck behind a desk answering the phone and ordering dildoes."

Taken off guard, Chevy laughed. They faced each other over coffee like friends. New friends. Lil was a hardworking country woman just like her, and they could really bond if time allowed.

Foster's offering me time. He's practically begging for it.

Lil took a sip of coffee. "Are you enjoying your stay?"

"Are you asking because it's your duty or because you really care?"

It was Lil's turn to chuckle. "Both."

"You can put in the survey that I'm thoroughly satisfied."

A light pink blush covered Lil's freckled cheeks. Apparently, the woman wasn't as open to the activities on this ranch or hearing about them as one would guess. Funny how a week ago, Chevy wasn't either. She'd just taken extreme measures to try to break a bad habit.

"But I do love the ranch. It's beautiful. You grew up here?"

That put Lil at ease, and they sat back and enjoyed their coffee and a good chat about cattle ranching.

"I heard you're responsible for saving my grazing land from the elk."

Now Chevy was the one blushing. "Just common sense."

"Not a lot of that anymore. It's an old-fashioned trait. Foster has it as well, which is why he's such an asset here."

"An asset to the ranch or The Boot Knockers?" She examined the woman closely.

Lil gave her a direct look that she returned.

Finally, Lil relaxed and wrapped her fingers around her mug. "I knew we'd lose Foster."

"What do you mean?"

"A bunch of the Texas Boot Knockers fell in love and left the group. Hugh and Riggs, the leaders, warned me of it."

"And were you directed to do anything about it?" Chevy shouldn't be sitting on the edge of her seat waiting for the answer, but she was.

"Am I going to try to squash whatever is budding between you and Foster? How can I? Who am I to dictate what people do in their lives? I just supply the land to run the operation. I don't necessarily agree with it."

"Interesting you say that. What does your family think?"

"What few of them are left don't know, and I don't care to share it. The townspeople give me some trouble over it now and then."

"That's unfair."

Lil nodded. "Foster's a good man, hardworking and level-headed. Over-educated but doesn't flaunt it."

She nodded. All this she knew.

"And he knows what he wants and goes after it." Lil eyed her meaningfully. Before Chevy could form a response, she got up and gave her a smile. "I've enjoyed chatting with you. I hope to do it again."

"Thank you. Me too." Chevy sat stunned as the woman walked away in long, purposeful strides. Did Lil mean more than her words reflected? Did she hope Chevy stuck around on the ranch and got to know Foster?

Damn. The sly rancher's a matchmaker.

* * * * *

The lodge bustled with all hands on deck. Boot Knockers streamed in and out the open double doors, carrying chairs and setting up long tables in the lodge's main hall.

"Where do you want these?" Bastian asked Foster, balancing a stack of chairs that would have crushed a lesser man.

Foster looked him over. Maybe he'd want to play with Chevy too. They could have a lot of fun if she decided to stick around longer. He wished she'd hurry up and say so—he was ready to burst with the need to know. He'd already cleared his schedule with Lil, so he didn't have any clients, but—

"Fos, these are mighty heavy."

"Sorry. Over there." He pointed the way, and Bastian walked away.

When Chevy had agreed to hold the wedding shower on the ranch, Foster had been about to thump himself on the back for a job well done. But the key to happiness with Miss Chevy was to sit back and let her steer the ship.

A strong woman deserved a right to exert her power, which she was doing in glorious form right now. She stood at the front of the room, directing everybody who came her direction. She threw herself into helping to configure the space according to her vision. And she was damn sexy in those fitted jeans and tank top.

She looked up and caught him drooling over her. With a shake of her head, she wagged her finger at him.

He gave her a wink and smile that had her lips popping open. He could almost hear her breathy sigh, and his cock stirred. He held her gaze another long, throbbing heartbeat until her attention was grabbed by a florist.

He looked around the room. She'd done a fabulous job, and if her sister didn't appreciate the hard work Chevy'd put in, then shame on her. His woman had really hit it out of the park, creating a dream atmosphere for the event.

Foster was keyed up about meeting her family too. He'd been in denial about that for most of the days leading up to the shower. He'd listened to her talk about aunts and how they lived closer to the ranch than Chevy's hometown where the original shower was to be held. He'd lain in bed next to her, listening to her talk to her mother and sister about the specifics, like catering menus and flowers.

Yeah, he was nervous as hell. Chevy had a history of collecting lousy boyfriends, and he didn't want to be roped into that stereotype. Besides, boyfriend seemed like such a silly word, and their relationship was anything but juvenile. When he looked at Chevy, he saw a future—a great one.

A crash from behind him made him spin. Glass shattered, and people jumped back to keep from being cut. A deliveryman stood there holding the other large, fancy glass jar that Chevy had carefully planned to use for a game.

Foster pivoted as she rushed past him. Oh damn. He wouldn't want on the receiving end of her anger. He stepped up to her side to run interference.

"I'm sorry, ma'am. It slipped," the deliveryman said.

Foster felt her draw a big breath and rested a hand on her spine to keep her from letting out her temper. But she composed herself and pinched the bridge of her nose. "It's over with and we'll get it cleaned up."

"My company will reimburse you."

"That's fine. We'll work it out later."

"Well, I can't believe my ears. My sister's been bossin' people around her whole life and now she's calm and accepting." The pretty brunette stuck out a hand to Foster. "I'm Sadie and I'm guessing you have something to do with taming a bit of Chevy's temper."

"Sadie." Chevy's tone was surprised and a warning all wrapped up in one.

"I'm Foster."

"Pleasure to meet you. I've heard a lot about you already."

Chevy flushed, and Foster couldn't stop the grin from spreading over his face. He liked that she'd told her family about him. Maybe it meant she was one step closer to being swayed to stay on the ranch with him.

Chevy stepped forward to hug her sister, and Foster gave them their moment. Then Sadie surprised him by hugging him around the neck. When she stepped away, he met Chevy's eye to see how she was taking this. He had no idea if she wanted to mix him with her family, but she was smiling.

Good.

With a weight off his shoulders, he leaned in to brush his lips over her cheek. "I'll get something to clean up the glass."

He felt her gaze following him and wondered what her sister was saying about him. He found a broom and dustpan. Then he got stopped twice to answer questions about the party. When he reached the spot again, Chevy and Sadie were gone. They were huddled with a few older ladies who must be relatives showing up early.

Someone jabbed him with an elbow, and he looked around. Lil stood a head shorter and wore the mischievous look of a little sister.

"What're you grinnin' about?" he asked.

"I'm glad to see you happy, Fos."

"You don't care that you're losing a Boot Knocker?"

"What would I care? That's for the new office manager to worry about. And you'll speak to Hugh and Riggs soon enough. They're in my office waiting for you."

"Oh shit." The prospect of facing those men and telling them he'd fallen for a client didn't give him warm fuzzy feelings. Rather, he felt the singe of what they'd say to him. Give him hell, tell him to leave the ranch.

But Lil wouldn't want that. She needed the help, and there wasn't any reason why he shouldn't stick around. Housing wasn't even an issue, because there were several rooms in the back of the lodge for employees.

"Guess I'll get it over with then."

"Set your mind at ease, cowboy."

"Is there any ease to be had in speaking with Hugh and Riggs?"

"Don't ask me. I'm just a *rancher*." She smiled widely about no longer being the office manager.

As nervous as he was, he returned her grin. "I'm happy for ya, Lil."

"Thank you kindly, cowboy. Now if you'll excuse me, I've got horses to see to. I suspect I'll hear how it goes with you."

"You will." He watched her walk away before turning to the office. When he was nervous, he often found himself ticking off the seconds by counting them. In this case, he counted his steps. The walk seemed to take forever, and he couldn't think of how to formulate the words he wanted to say to the two big bosses.

I've decided being a Boot Knocker isn't for me.

I've made a mistake.

Except it wasn't a mistake—far from it. Chevy was the most right thing he'd known besides coming to this ranch. *I'm supposed to be here, just not as a Boot Knocker.*

He wrapped his fingers around the door handle and pulled it open with a sigh. He'd never sweat about a job in his life, but this one had meant something to him. It had afforded him freedom to work as he pleased and to help prove to women they were worth his time.

He could start by telling that to Hugh and Riggs. They of all people would understand, having started as Boot Knockers themselves. They'd been lovers and then when a special woman came along, it was all over for them.

I've met someone special, he thought of telling them. *And I can't lay a hand on another woman besides Chevy.*

The office was set up with a seating area, and strangely enough, the bosses were lounging there. They sat in adjacent chairs, Hugh with his legs stretched out reading a local newspaper and Riggs with his ankle hitched over his knee looking over the Montana Boot Knockers' promotional packet.

"Do you think the wording here's right?" he asked, putting a finger over a bit of text.

"Hm?" Hugh looked up, distracted. "Let me see." He leaned over and Riggs held out the pamphlet.

"Our marketing department spent weeks making sure that booklet conveys everything we want it to. What do you find odd about it?"

"The—" Riggs noticed Foster standing there.

He squared his shoulders in the face of Riggs' dark stare. It had to be Foster's imagination that the man was looking into his soul and seeing everything he hadn't yet figured out how to say.

"Welcome to the party," Hugh said, getting to his feet to shake Foster's hand. Riggs did the same.

"Should we go into the office?" Foster asked. *And get this over with?*

"Nah, I'm comfy right here." Hugh settled again, and Riggs took up his former seat. Foster dropped into a chair across from them with a coffee table as buffer between them. The solid oak seemed like a good shield too, in a pinch.

Hugh set aside his newspaper and adopted the same pose as his lover. Did he even realize how alike they were? Living together, sharing the same woman, probably did that.

Foster's mind flitted over these details as a way to keep it from the conversation. He was no coward, but he hated letting down people who'd given him a chance. He'd loved his job and made the best money of his life. But now he'd found something worth moving on for.

Riggs gave a resigned sigh. "He looks like all the others, man," he said to Hugh.

Foster held his own under those two stares, but he couldn't say he wasn't sweating a bit. They were like big brothers who disapproved of his behavior.

Finally, Hugh sighed too. "Damn, is it true then?"

"Is what true?" Foster gripped the arm of the chair.

"You fell for a client?"

Well, at least it was all out in the open in one swift sentence.

He nodded.

"You know there's often infatuation that comes with this job. It's temporary," Riggs said.

"This isn't temporary."

"You haven't had enough time to know if it's temporary infatuation and lust." Hugh leaned back and, elbows on the arms of his chair and his fingers templed on his lap.

Foster leaned forward. "Was that how you felt when Sybill came to the ranch as a client? That what you had was temporary?"

"Fuck," Riggs said softly.

Hugh's expression didn't change from his thoughtful study of Foster. He straightened his back and waited for the answer.

At last, Hugh pursed his lips. "No. We knew the difference right away."

Foster let out a breath he hadn't realized he'd been holding. "Exactly."

"This woman returns the feelings?"

"I… I don't know exactly. She hasn't said it straight up." For the first time, Foster wondered if he was jumping to conclusions, jumping the gun, jumping into a kettle of boiling water. If she didn't want the same thing he did, and he'd just admitted it to all to his bosses, then they wouldn't trust him again. He might be let go of this job *and* lose the girl.

Chevy had only committed to the shower. Between planning it, they'd had some amazing strolls around the ranch, worked hard to put in a new enclosure for the next batch of spring calves and talked a lot. Not to mention the mind-blowing sex.

But she hadn't once told him she felt as strongly as he did. Told him she was confused, yes. Wanted to go slow, for sure.

Hell.

They all fell silent.

"I think the only answer is to call her in here," Hugh said.

Foster shook his head. "I draw the line at that. This is my work and my problem. She's busy with her sister's wedding shower and we aren't troubling her." He squared his shoulders and looked the men in the eye. "No matter what she feels, I know that I've changed. I can't go on being a Boot Knocker in that capacity. Now, I can run the backside of this operation, manage the guys so to speak. And work the ranch. There's plenty to do with the new cabins to build and the crew to expand you mentioned last time you were up."

Hugh and Riggs exchanged a look.

"I know this place inside and out. I can hire new Boot Knockers and see to it that everything runs smoothly."

"Can you keep the same thing that happened to you from happening to them?"

"Could you down in Texas? You've lost what—six or seven guys now?"

Hugh grunted.

Riggs touched his lover's arm. "It's a turnover rate we must accept. The important thing is to keep a group of up-and-comers to fill those spots on hand." He raised his jaw toward Foster. "He could do that."

Hugh gazed at Foster a long second. Then he sat back against his seat. "Fine. It's the best solution at the moment, but I won't say this isn't a hard loss, Foster. We had high hopes for you. In the six months since we've started, you've gotten the most acclaim here in Montana."

Foster found a grin tugging at the corner of his lips. "Funny how my woman didn't give a damn about any of that. Actually, she came here so I could *not* give her the slick treatment I gave all the rest."

"Figures. Women can be contrary creatures. Sybill's led us for a merry chase but it's what keeps the spice in the relationship." Riggs' expression reflected the love for their leading lady.

"I guess this means we'll be working more closely together." Hugh stuck out his hand. "Welcome to the administrative side of things. And don't fuck it up with Chevy."

"Thank you, guys. Have no intention of it."

* * * * *

Chevy picked up a flute of sparkling champagne with blueberries bobbing in it and brought it to her lips. The alcohol was light and refreshing. And the first thing that came to mind was how much Foster would enjoy tasting it on her lips.

Her tongue.

She glanced around for him but he was nowhere in sight. He'd vanished near the end of the setup of the space, and she'd been too involved with decorations and seating charts to go and find him.

But... she missed him.

Seeing her sister so happy, surrounded by family here to share the joy of her future, made Chevy think about her own.

Her extended time on the ranch hadn't given her the time she needed to decide if she wanted to let down her wall and give herself to Foster. He was waiting for it—she saw it in the way he watched her so closely, as if he was about to say something but bit it off.

It wasn't fair of her not to give them as much of her energy as he had. The man had lived for her alone these past few days. And she could easily see how this would be his way of life from here on. When he was with her, she really did feel adored, cherished. All those things she'd ached for and that had gotten her into trouble with the men of her past.

She sipped her champagne and looked on as Sadie was given big, enveloping hugs and well wishes by a group of Michael's cousins who were taking leave.

"Beautiful venue. That view is amazing. How did you ever find it?" The woman at her side was a distant relative of Michael's too. Sadie hadn't been kidding when she'd said he had a huge family.

"It was a last-minute find."

"And a gem of one too. Well done, Chevy. I'll see you at the wedding. I'm sure it will be just as marvelous." The lady smiled and Chevy returned it.

Then she stood alone again. She finished off her champagne and considered gulping the berries from the bottom of the glass but thought it would be rude. Later maybe she'd come back and get a plate of berries and corner her lover. Eating off his hard, chiseled body was definitely something that inspired a thrill deep in her belly.

She glanced around at the doors again, hoping to see him strolling through them, tall and confident, his hat sitting low and his jeans lower on his hips. Her fingers clenched at the thought of grabbing those hard buns of his and dragging him against her.

Okay, it was time for her to stop being a wuss and face her emotions for the Boot Knocker. She had no idea how it had happened, but she wanted more of him. To wake up with him in the mornings, ride the fields at noon and burn for each other all night long.

She'd fallen for him so hard, she'd never bounce back from this one if he decided to dump her. Her first instinct was to walk away, to do the dumping. But just the thought of leaving Foster made her ache.

Suddenly her sister stood before her, beaming. "A lot of people are leaving. Come say goodbye with me." Then she looked more closely at Chevy. "What's wrong?"

"Just thinking."

"Are you thinking about that sexy cowboy of yours? I would be too—he's gorgeous."

Chevy let out a shaky breath. "Actually, yes, I am."

"Forget about saying goodbye to my guests. You've more than done your part today, and I'll never be able to tell you how amazing this day has been or how thankful I am that I shared it with you." She leaned in and kissed Chevy's cheek. "Now go find your cowboy and tell him what you're thinking about. I can see you want to."

Chevy's legs carried her to the door before she realized she'd made a decision to go. Once she pushed open the heavy glass door and burst into the warm Montana day, a sense of freedom hit.

She wore a sundress and high heels but that didn't stop her from jogging around the building toward the cabin where she and Foster had been staying together. Holed up for the steamiest nights of her life. They'd fallen into the habit of talking for hours after making love. That was something she'd never had with her past boyfriends.

Adrenaline made her fingers tingle. She rounded the corner at a faster clip and was snagged around the middle. Swung off her feet and pinned against the wall of the lodge, a huge chest flattening her breasts.

249

She sucked in a startled gasp, and he slammed his lips over hers. The dark, musky flavors were all man. All Foster.

She parted her lips and he slipped his tongue inside. He groaned and she answered with a throaty moan. She raised her hands to cup his face, angling her own head to give him complete access.

He plundered her mouth for long minutes, deepening the passes and then backed off to nip at her lips. He bit into her bottom one and dragged her close. They started all over again.

And his hands. God, his hands. He knew exactly where to touch her to bring her heat to the surface.

Callused fingers trailed over her bare arms. Gripped her hands and planted them to her sides while he rocked his hips against hers. Need spiraled out of control. Small noises escaped her, and she hoped they didn't carry on the air around to the front of the lodge where Sadie's guests were saying their goodbyes.

Passion ruled her, and she gave into it with a leap of her heart. This was Foster, not some crappy guy who'd tried to sweet-talk her until he tired of her. Foster already knew more about her than all of them put together, after only a couple weeks.

"Foster, stop," she panted.

He kissed a path down her throat to the tops of her breasts, too involved to take notice of her request.

She freed her hands and cradled his jaw. Lifting his head, she looked into his eyes. "Wait."

His gaze burned so hot, liquid heat soaked her panties. "What's wrong?"

"Nothing. I just…" How to say she wanted him to take her—all of her? Maybe the words were overrated anyway. She'd show him instead.

She caught his hand and pressed it up under her skirt. He groaned as he touched her damp panties. Immediately, he slid his fingers under the elastic and found her throbbing clit.

Gasping, she let her head fall back against the wall. The view of the ranch swam before her eyes a second before she closed them on the bliss that was Foster's fingers.

He circled her nubbin, painting her own juices over it until the nerves snapped. She curled into his touch, small pleas leaving her.

"Take me. Have it all."

"Right here, baby doll?" His voice was a low, urgent growl. "You want me to fuck you against the wall with your people just around that corner?"

"Yes, I need it. Please."

She'd barely gotten the words out when he moved his hand from her pussy to work at his fly. He tore it open in a few brief heartbeats and somehow managed a condom too. Soon she'd have to tell him she was on the pill and had a clean bill of health. If they were going to be a couple, she didn't want to always have the barrier between them.

Joy flooded her as he nudged her thighs higher apart and speared her in his hot gaze. "I've never wanted a woman like I want you. Feel how fucking hard I am for you?" He pressed the tip of his cock against her slick folds.

"Yes," she whimpered. "Oh God, yes. Now, Foster!"

He jerked his hips and filled her in one smooth glide. She'd hardly stretched around his length before he was moving within her. Cushioning the back of her head with one broad palm as he fucked her against the wall. The wildness of it all gave her an erotic push toward the edge of release. She teetered there as he circled his hips and pumped into her.

"So fucking tight. What have you been thinking about in that shower, baby doll?"

"This. All this." She spread her hands over his shoulders and up to his angular jaw. She kissed him with a new fervor as he bottomed out in her and sent her sailing.

* * * * *

Fuck, she was coming on his cock. He watched ecstasy claim her beautiful features and let her panting moans take over his control. He crushed his lips to hers and their tongues tangled.

Oh yes, this was right. He could have a piece of heaven right here with Chevy on this ranch. Live out their days until they were able to get a place of their own, maybe a small spot tucked up in the foothills. A good place to raise cattle — and kids.

He wanted a family with her. Hell, there wasn't a single thing he didn't want with this woman.

His cock head stretched to the deepest reaches of her tight heat. Her breasts were bulging from the bodice of her sundress, the tanned globes inviting his tongue. He kissed one, then the other. And after two more churns of his hips, he tensed.

A burning need rushed up from the base of his spine. He stiffened, growled into her throat and came in a mindless explosion.

She hung in his hold, small whimpers still escaping her. He kissed them away one at a time. Each press of his lips growing softer and more tender with feeling.

"I quit my job, Chevy."

She twitched back to look at him, which wasn't very far when she was pinned to the wall. "Are you serious?"

"As a heart attack. I can't lay a hand on another woman, baby doll. You're it for me. Even though I haven't known you very long, I know you're all I want."

"Oh Foster…" She leaned her forehead against his and her eyes fluttered shut. His heart pounded with the seconds, counting them off until she spoke. It didn't take long for her response.

She opened her eyes and met his gaze. "I want you. I've known it but been too afraid to admit it. I don't know what will happen or how things will work between us, but I want to try. Like you said, we deserve to explore what's between us."

He rocked his hips into her, and her inner muscles gripped at his cock all over again.

"Against the wall for a second time?" she asked.

"Nah, can't have you getting bored with me. I thought I'd take you around front and we could do it for your whole family."

She pinched his ear hard enough to sting, and he yelped a laugh. "You've made me question my standards. I never thought I'd be having sex in a pond or against a wall."

"There's a lot more to come, baby doll."

"I can only fantasize."

"No need. We'll get started right away. You finished here with the shower?"

She nodded.

"Good, because I'm taking you back to the cabin. I've got a candlestick with your name on it."

She made a noise of disapproval. "Not cheesy candlelight sex."

He arched a brow at her. "Who said that's what I had planned with the candle?" He plunged his cock deep into her again, giving her a good enough idea that her eyes widened.

His chest couldn't be any warmer, his heart fuller. She'd agreed to give them a shot.

And he was going to spend every day of his life showing her how damn serious he was about her.

Epilogue

Chevy held up her champagne flute in a toast to the bride and groom. Sadie and Michael stood at the center of the table facing everyone. They both beamed with happiness. Sadie had never looked so beautiful, and the inner joy she radiated made Chevy realize she'd been wrong about Michael. They were perfect together.

"To Sadie and Michael," the best man said.

Everyone echoed it, and Chevy took a sip of her champagne. Her gaze landed heavily on the one man in the whole place that she wanted to be with right now. She couldn't wait to get away from the head table and be in Foster's arms.

The past two months had been a whirlwind of time spent on The Boot Knockers Ranch together. They'd even spent a weekend or two here on her own turf. Foster and her father had talked about cattle nonstop, and she'd seen her mother give her an approving look more than once.

But what really mattered to Chevy was how her own feelings had changed. She'd gone to Foster's bed as a skeptic and come out knowing she wanted more with him. Much more.

She was head over boots for the hunky cowboy.

He raised his glass to her and then brought it to her lips. She got up, gathering her long gown in her hand so she wouldn't get her sparkly heels tangled in it, and moved toward him.

He met her halfway and she appraised him in his fine attire. The suit fit him like a second skin.

"Looking dashing, Foster."

"For a cowboy. Is this better than the Wranglers?"

"No. The jeans are far hotter. Though I won't complain about peeling this suit off you."

"I feel the same about your dress." He slid a hand around her waist, over the satin. It slipped against her skin deliciously, giving her thoughts of taking it off right now.

He hovered an inch from her mouth. "Let's find someplace we can be alone."

She shot a look around. Her sister was occupied with her new husband and the guests wouldn't care if she was gone. She nodded.

Foster's crooked bad-boy smile made her second-guess his motives for getting her alone, though.

He took her by the hand and led her out of the posh space. Her sister had gotten the perfect day, not a cloud in the sky, to herald her union with Michael. The sun kissed Chevy's face, and she tipped it up.

"You're beautiful, you know."

She smiled at the man at her side. "You're pretty gorgeous yourself."

He flashed those wicked white teeth that undid her every time and towed her around the side of the building to a gazebo. Running beside it was a small stream with an arched bridge over it where she and the wedding party had taken a gazillion photos earlier.

When they were in the cooler shade of the gazebo, Foster turned to her and caught her hands.

A spike of excitement hit her belly. The look on his face…

Suddenly, he dropped to one knee.

She gasped. "Foster…"

He stared into her eyes. "Will you do me the honor…"

She waited, hardly breathing, her world spinning out of control. He was about to propose to her at her own sister's wedding.

"Of letting me pull up this beautiful gown and eat your pussy?"

Caught off guard, she threw back her head and laughed. She caught his smile and a promise in his eyes.

She skimmed the angle of his jaw with her fingertips. "Oh yes."

She didn't even look around to see if anybody was about as he inched up her skirt and buried his tongue between her thighs. The exquisite pleasure of his tongue moving over her heated flesh made her shake. She forgot about his twisted humor and how she wasn't getting a proposal, because in time she knew they'd end up at the altar just like her sister and Michael.

Every pass of his tongue sent white-hot need through Chevy's body. Her knees threatened to buckle and her bodice felt far too constricting. She wanted her nipples pinched between his fingers as he drew moan after moan from her.

"Oh yessss. Yes, it's so good."

He sank his tongue deep and then pulled it free to circle her clit again. She was on the edge, shaking with the need to come.

He stroked her hand and something moved up her finger. She blinked through the haze of sexual pleasure to look down at her hand.

Where a platinum band with a fat diamond now sat.

Before she could respond, he ran his tongue over the taut bundle of her nerves and her orgasm hit. Her body convulsed in his hold as he trapped her clit under his tongue and drew out her pulsations. Then he took his sweet time gathering all her juices.

She rocked one final time into his mouth and looked down at his smiling face, his lips glistening with her wetness.

"What kind of proposal was that?"

"I hope a memorable one, seein' how it'll be your only one." He clutched her hands and ran his thumb over the platinum band and the bump of the diamond. "Chevy, will you be my wife?"

She cocked her head. "If you promise to do that every day, then yes."

It was his turn to be caught off guard. He barked a laugh and got to his feet, letting her gown fall back into place. Then he cupped her face gently and stared into her eyes.

"Seriously, you'll marry me?" he asked, all play gone from his features.

Her heart rolled over with pure love for this cowboy. She wrapped her arms around his neck. "Yes, Foster. I'm so excited to spend the rest of my life with you. So excited that I'm shaking."

"Nah, that's because you just came all over my tongue, baby doll."

She giggled. "Seems to me I should make you shake with excitement too." She reached for his sleek black belt holding up his suit pants.

"I can't deny my fiancée anything, now can I?" He turned his back to the world and held her gaze as she dropped to her knees and gave him the memory of a lifetime.

Read on for a sneak peek at The Boot Knocker's Baby.

"Wyoming bets twenty grand in peanuts. He's all in. No, wait. He's got a stash in his lap. He's holding out on us, folks." Shayne's commentary roused a few chuckles from The Boot Knockers circling the poker table, but many remained stoic.

Wyoming gave him a crooked grin that could mean he was holding all the right cards or none of them.

"The man's not raising his bet, folks. The poker faces are fierce tonight. We must have a lot of hungry guys here. They're not giving up a single peanut. Didn't any of you get dinner or what?"

Foster sat back in his seat, ending his game. "No dinner for me. But I've got a tasty morsel waiting for me in my cabin, so I'll catch y'all tomorrow." He was the only man among them who had a real relationship. He stood and swiped his peanuts off the table. He shoved them in his pockets and headed for the door.

A few comments like "pussy-whipped" followed him but Foster just gave them the finger before the door shut behind him.

Shayne, acting as dealer, stared between his buddies. The weekly poker game was a prelude to the upcoming week of fun when the new batch of women arrived at the ranch. Shayne was off this week, though, and that meant he'd be working double-time around the place.

He didn't mind. It kept his mind off things.

He folded his arms on the table and stared down the others still in the game. "What's it gonna be, Nolan? Rock?"

Nolan picked up the pile of peanuts in front of him and dropped them on the table in a repetitive noise that usually, by the end of the night, got on Shayne's nerves. But he wasn't all that eager to return to his bunk alone, so he ignored it for the time being.

Rock, the math nerd of the group, peered at them from under the brim of his cowboy hat and pushed up his glasses using a forefinger. The chicks fell all over him, and Shayne had been surprised at first to see how many preferred the smart type.

Rock was also a Dom on the ranch. His skill with ropes and whips surpassed his knowledge of numbers, and every woman left very, very satisfied.

264

Shayne had been on the receiving end of Rock's paddle once, just to say he'd done it, and he'd never been the same since. He definitely had an appreciation for the art of BDSM, though he didn't go nearly that far with his own ladies.

The ranch specialized in treating women with sexual hang-ups or body issues, but Shayne was paired with a lot of virgins. He knew how to put a woman at ease, work her up… and finally show her the real fireworks.

He was growing hard thinking about one particular virgin he'd bedded. Those sweet, raspy cries…

Damn, now he was going to have blue-balls for a solid seven days unless one of the other guys shared. His mind kept spinning back to that one sassy and sweet thing from his past.

He liked his women sharp like her. Since Jolie, he'd had a preference for smart girls.

He pushed out a sigh and snapped at the guys. "You gonna play this hand all day or make a damn move?"

Wyoming swung his gaze up to him and arched a brow. "You got somewhere better to be, Shayne?"

He filled his lungs to the fullest and held his breath for five heartbeats. When he released the air, he wasn't any less jittery. Damn, why had he let his mind wander to Jolie? His last real relationship before coming to the ranch almost two years before kept surfacing like groundhog holes on a prairie. Hell, he even dreamed about her some nights.

He clenched his jaw and waited. Summoning the patience to finish the poker game and get out of here before anyone caught him sulking.

Or whatever he wanted to call it. He hated the dark weight he often felt when thinking of Jolie. She'd been too young, too committed to her nursing degree and her dreams for her future to mess around with a dumb cowboy like him.

Plus, he'd wanted out of that small town in Montana more than anything. He considered himself a mountain man, and he'd been born and raised in what was just about the only lowlands in the damn state. That was his luck.

Another reason he was dealing, not betting peanuts.

Wyoming pushed back from the table. "Take all I got, boys. I have the shittiest hand in the house."

"Let's see." Nolan leaned close to Wyoming and licked his ear.

"Keep that up and you'll see something besides cards, man." Wyoming didn't bother to swipe off the saliva. He just gave Nolan an appraising look. Wyoming was a kinky fuck. He liked men, women and all pairings in between. Shayne wouldn't be surprised if the two disappeared after the game.

Wyoming looked between each of the guys. Only Rock didn't look nervous. Then again, he never did.

"Show your hand," Shayne said.

Wyoming flipped his cards to reveal a full house.

"Fuck." Nolan tossed a peanut at Wyoming. It bounced off his pec and to the table. Wyoming plucked it up and crushed the shell with a pinch of thumb and forefinger. Then he tossed the little nuts into his mouth and chewed around a grin.

"Bag these all up for me, boys. I'll be by to collect my winnings in the morning. Nolan? You comin'?"

Several whistles sounded as the pair left the barn. Shayne stood and stretched. His back creaked. He wasn't used to sitting for so long. "I'm out too."

The other Boot Knockers stood as well.

"Who's bagging up Wyoming's nuts?" Rock asked.

Shayne cocked a grin. "That would be Nolan." The remaining guys laughed as they left the barn without a backward glance.

When Shayne inhaled the fresh Montana night air, he caught the hint of the mountains. People didn't believe him when he swore he could smell the mountains, the earth and snow. Okay, maybe he was a little off his rocker. But the mountains called to him.

He faced the ridge that would take him up and over the mountains in the east. He could pack the saddlebags and set off on horseback. A week of solitude and living rough off the land appealed like nothing else did.

He couldn't shirk his work, but he might get a day to head up into higher elevations and try to find some semblance of calm.

For months, he'd been thinking of doing this, just to see if he could lay Jolie's ghost to rest. The woman shouldn't have any hold on him at all. He hadn't seen or heard from her since walking out. She'd told him she understood his need to pursue his own happiness, though her lower lip had quivered.

Dammit. He was doing it again.

He set off in search of his bunk. Sleep would end his thoughts—but then there were the dreams to contend with. As he passed a shadowed spot behind the barn, he heard a quiet grunt and rustle of clothing. He grinned. So Wyoming and Nolan hadn't even made it as far as a cabin before seeking pleasure.

He could stick around and watch or join in. But it wouldn't fight off his demons for long.

He needed the mountains. But what he thought about at night when he was loneliest was a pretty little woman, smart and as classy as Miss Montana, though she cussed a little.

He smiled wider at the echoes of her going off on a tangent. She'd been too good for him, deserved much more than he could give. Beyond being good in the sack, what did he have to offer?

1-click The Boot Knocker's Baby
on Amazon

Em Petrova

Em Petrova is a USA Today Bestselling Author who was raised by hippies in the wilds of Pennsylvania but told her parents at the age of four she wanted to be a gypsy when she grew up. She has a soft spot for babies, puppies and 90s Grunge music and believes in Bigfoot and aliens. She started writing at the age of twelve and prides herself on making her characters larger than life and her sex scenes hotter than hot.

She burst into the world of publishing in 2010 after having five beautiful bambinos and figuring they were old enough to get their own snacks while she pounds away at the keys. In her not-so-spare time, she is fur-mommy to a Labradoodle named Daisy Hasselhoff.

Find Em Petrova at empetrova.com

Other Titles by Em Petrova

SEAL Team Blackout

271

WEST Protection

NORTH OF LOVE
XTREME RULES

Crossroads
BAD IN BOOTS
CONFIDENT IN CHAPS
COCKY IN A COWBOY HAT
SAVAGE IN A STETSON
SHOW-OFF IN SPURS

Dark Falcons MC
DIXON
TANK
PATRIOT
DIESEL
BLADE

The Guard
HIS TO SHELTER
HIS TO DEFEND
HIS TO PROTECT

Moon Ranch

SOMETHING ABOUT A BOUNTY HUNTER
SOMETHING ABOUT A MOUNTAIN MAN

Operation Cowboy Series
KICKIN' UP DUST
SPURS AND SURRENDER

The Boot Knockers Ranch Series
PUSHIN' BUTTONS
BODY LANGUAGE
REINING MEN
ROPIN' HEARTS
ROPE BURN
COWBOY NOT INCLUDED
COWBOY BY CANDLELIGHT
THE BOOT KNOCKER'S BABY
ROPIN' A ROMEO
WINNING WYOMING

Ménage à Trouble Series
WRANGLED UP
UP FOR GRABS
HOOKING UP
ALL WOUND UP

DOUBLED UP novella duet
UP CLOSE
WARMED UP

Another Shot at Love Series
GRIFFIN
BRANT
AXEL

Rope 'n Ride Series
BUCK
RYDER
RIDGE
WEST
LANE
WYNONNA

The Dalton Boys
COWBOY CRAZY Hank's story
COWBOY BARGAIN Cash's story
COWBOY CRUSHIN' Witt's story
COWBOY SECRET Beck's story
COWBOY RUSH Kade's Story
COWBOY MISTLETOE a Christmas novella

277

COWBOY FLIRTATION Ford's story
COWBOY TEMPTATION Easton's story
COWBOY SURPRISE Justus's story
COWGIRL DREAMER Gracie's story
COWGIRL MIRACLE Jessamine's story
COWGIRL HEART Kezziah's story

Single Titles and Boxes
THE BOOT KNOCKERS RANCH BOX SET
THE DALTON BOYS BOX SET
SINFUL HEARTS
JINGLE BOOTS
A COWBOY FOR CHRISTMAS
FULL RIDE

Firehouse 5 Series
ONE FIERY NIGHT
CONTROLLED BURN
SMOLDERING HEARTS

Hardworking Heroes Novellas

EM PETROVA
USA TODAY BESTSELLING AUTHOR

Made in United States
North Haven, CT
26 April 2024

51810067R00157